Contents

About the Author

Keith Taylor is the true identity of the million plus selling author behind the pen names Aya Fukunishi and K A Taylor, who toiled for years writing trashy but bizarrely popular romance novels that you absolutely shouldn't ever read, not even to satisfy your curiosity. Not even on a dare. Just don't do it. You'll never get that time back.

Throughout those long, cold years in the romance trenches Keith secretly longed to return to his first love and true calling: explosively awesome post-apocalyptic fiction. The bestselling Last Man Standing series was written in the months after he finally realized he couldn't write one more damned love story. He moved back to his writing bunker in Mongolia, disconnected from the world and returned with HUNGER and CORDYCEPS, and is now hard at work on book three, VACCINE.

Taylor hails from the rainy suburbs of Manchester in the north of England. He lives with his wife, Otgontsetseg, and splits his time between Ulaanbaatar, Mongolia and Bangkok, Thailand. He's been deported from more than one country, once spent two months living in his car, has crapped in the wilderness everywhere from the Gobi Desert to the Pamir mountains on the Afghan border and survives on a diet of meat, cheese, beer and cigarettes. He probably shouldn't still be alive, but for now appears to be unkillable.

Website: **authorkeithtaylor.com**

For news about upcoming releases, sales and various other nonsense you can follow Keith on Facebook:

facebook.com/keithtaylorauthor

or subscribe to his mailing list:

app.mailerlite.com/webforms/landing/y1i5 k1

Last Man Standing: HUNGER

by

Keith Taylor

The following is a rough draft of an article of mine that appeared in the October 2017 issue of Time Magazine, recovered from an old USB stick I found stuck to a chewed piece of gum in the lining of my jacket.

This was the last thing I was ever paid to write, and my first article in an international magazine. The final printed version - with the cursing removed and a couple of paragraphs switched around - is still out there somewhere, but it's probably not worth sifting through the ruins of America to find it.

Last Man Standing

Thomas Freeman

"There's another thing they don't show in the movies," Paul chuckles bitterly, playing with the moist, half peeled label on his sweating bottle of Singha. "The bathroom arrangements. I spent three weeks stuck in that damned apartment, and by the end I was about ready to throw myself off the balcony just to escape the smell."

I wrinkle my nose and nod sympathetically. Even now you can't go anywhere in Thailand without experiencing the intensely *human* odor of five million refugees and not nearly enough bathrooms. The air is infused with the hot, cloying stink of excrement, and in the camps the gutters run blue with the residue of countless leaking chemical toilets.

"Reminded me of the time we spent a month dog-sitting for Zaya in Ulaanbaatar. You remember that?" he asks. "What was it, January 2013? Minus forty degrees outside, and as soon as the dog took a shit on the balcony it froze solid." The carefully peeled label tears in half between his fingers and he rips it angrily from the bottle, his face locked in a violent scowl.

Paul's pent up frustration is palpable, quite intimidating and entirely out of character. Those who know him (full disclosure: I've known Mr. McQueen socially for a little more than five years) would invariably describe him as a gentle giant, his actions always measured and his voice unusually soft as if to compensate for the implicit threat of his hulking frame. The man in front of me looks as if he's struggling to resist the urge to punch someone. This is not the Paul McQueen I used to know.

"Couldn't get rid of it with a paint scraper, it was so frozen," He tears the paper to scraps as he speaks, in a way that makes me wonder if he's even conscious he's doing it. I look down at his fingers and notice the nails are bitten down to the quick with traces of blood at the edges where he's nervously gnawed at them. "When that first warm morning arrived a month's worth of shit defrosted like a bowl of ice cream. The smell was so bad Ogi had to move in with her sister for a week."

I nod again, urging him on. "And you had the heat, of course. Must have been even worse." I pull a sour face, almost gagging at the thought.

"*Jesus*, the heat. April in Bangkok. Hottest month of the year, and no AC once the power went out. It probably wouldn't have been so bad if I'd been staying in one of the big new tower blocks with a little breeze, but our place was..." He shakes his head. "Well, you remember our old place at Sutti Mansion, right? $250 a month, and nothing in front of the balcony but the wall of the building next door. We used to have to run the fan 24/7 just to keep it below 100 degrees. I guess it wasn't the smartest thing to do, shitting in the only place with a hint of fresh air. Still, you live and learn..." Paul sighs and stares at his bottle for a moment.

"Well, some of us do."

He drains his beer and waves the empty bottle in the direction of the waitress. He either doesn't notice or doesn't care that it catches the lip of the glass bowl of bar snacks, sending nuts and glittering shards crashing to the tile floor. The pretty bar girl quickly scurries along with dustpan and brush, and Paul stares covetously at my drink as she sweeps unnoticed beneath his feet.

"Mind if I...?" He picks up my bottle before waiting for an answer, draining the lukewarm beer in one pull.

"Please, go on. Tell me how it started." I shoot an apologetic glance at the waitress but she doesn't look up from the broken glass. I get the impression she's become accustomed to Paul's drunken behavior over the past month.

"Well, I'm sure you know what the Thais tell you, about the Iranians smuggling in some sort of chemical weapons? I take it you haven't come all this way to hear the fairytale, right? All this shit came a couple of months after some inept Iranian fuckers accidentally blew themselves to pieces up in Ekamai, so the Arabs made good scapegoats when it all went to shit. No, that bullshit story may play back in the States, but I was there. I saw how it started, and since I'm the only one who saw it start and made out alive I'm... well, I'm uniquely qualified. I'm done lying about it."

"You mean it wasn't a chemical attack?" I'm on the edge of my seat. Paul was cagey and evasive in the emails we exchanged over the last few weeks, usually sent late at night after he'd returned home from the bar. He implied that there was something amiss with the popular narrative, but this is the first time he's gone on record with a claim that the Iranians may not have been responsible.

"No, I'm not saying it wasn't chemical," he continues, shaking his head. "I'm just saying it didn't happen like they said. There sure as shit wasn't a fleet of trucks spraying down the streets with toxins and blasting readings of the Koran like a fucking ice cream van tune. I was there when the first of them turned, and I know it started in one place: Sala fucking Daeng. All the outbreaks later up on Sukhumvit came from the trains."

I look down at my notes, but can't find the right page. Paul's claims would later seem accurate, according to Twitter and Facebook archives reconstructed in the days after the outbreak and reported by Al Jazeera. The first social media reports came from the Silom area at Sala Daeng, a station on the BTS line in Bangkok's central business district, at 14:32. Seventeen minutes later tweets began to flood in from around the stations further to the north and south. They radiated out along the BTS and MRT lines (the overhead and underground train lines that served central Bangkok) for a little more than twenty minutes before the cell networks became overloaded with traffic and the 4G signal dropped out.

Songkran is too crazy for me this year. Lots of fights on Silom Road. Heading home.

*Text translated from the original Thai. The tweet was accompanied by a blurred photo that appears to have been taken through the window of the McDonalds at the south end of the road, around 50 feet from the bulk of the crowd. The photo clearly shows a teen boy biting a middle aged woman on the thigh.

"I didn't even want to be there, to be honest. I was too old for water fights two decades ago, and the idea of getting doused with dirty water by a few thousand drunk kids didn't sound like my idea of a fun Saturday. You ever spend time in Bangkok during Songkran?"

I shake my head. This had been my first visit to Thailand, and I'd been working on a story on illegal logging up in Vientiane, Laos in the week before Bangkok fell.

"It's a disgrace. It used to be traditional to wash your shrines and images of Buddha with fragranced water during Thai new year, but over the years that nice little tradition somehow turned into a drunken week long water fight. Every year hundreds die in drink driving accidents, and already there'd been a few murders in the city. Some guy got drenched on the way to a funeral, got into a rumble with a drunk kid and ended up stabbed in the chest. Another guy was beaten to death when he got a little handsy with some bloke's sister in a crowd. It gets worse every year.

"Now Sala Daeng, that's Songkran ground central in Bangkok. They shut down a section of Silom Road, everyone loads up on cheap booze and for days the whole street becomes a huge party. Thousands of people chuck buckets of water at each other, spray each other with water guns and throw around a ton of minty chalk shit. Not sure what it is, but *that* was what started it."

I frown, confused. "How do you mean?"

"It's the powder they throw at each other. It's like... what do you call it, talcum powder, but it smells like mint. They love to soak you with water then cake you with the stuff. Nasty shit at the best of times, but this stuff was different. This was bright yellow, like turmeric. Nobody else was throwing yellow shit, and from where I was standing up on the flyover I could see exactly what was happening. There was this weird little group of people in the middle of the action, white folks dressed like they'd just come from church, with heads shaved clean like Buddhist monks. They were the ones throwing the yellow stuff, and everywhere they threw it people started acting like they'd been hit with tear gas, trying to blink it out of their eyes. It was like the stuff was burning their skin. A few people fell to the ground, and the rest tried to pour water in their eyes to clear them. Too late, of course. It all went to shit pretty quickly after that. Thank you, my dear."

These last words are to the waitress, who sets down two fresh bottles wrapped in foam coolers (*beer condoms*, as Paul once described them). He hands over a wad of cash, tipping the waitress heavily, and lifts his bottle unsteadily. He'd been drinking for hours before I arrived, and after taking a long pull on the ice cold beer he excuses himself, pushes back his chair and stumbles unsteadily towards the men's room.

At 1,000 baht (around $35) a bottle, Paul is one of the few who can still enjoy the dwindling supply of Thai beer here in the interim capital of Hua Hin. He's done the rounds on the morning shows, popping up via satellite on news broadcasts around the world to support the official story of the Thai government, a job for which he's been paid well. Not a day has gone by in the last two months without this handsome, square jawed Australian appearing on our screens to rail against the Iranians, telling the same story of a massive terrorist attack; of white vans roaming the streets, spraying down the sidewalks with a fine mist. He spoke of masked 'Arabs' (his word, not mine) throwing what he described as tear gas canisters into crowds of civilians.

The new military junta has used him as a tool, hailing him as a hero for his escape from the dead city. He fought bravely through a million-strong crowd of the walking dead to bring word of the Islamic terrorists to the wider world, and his story has served to bolster support for the new government both at home and abroad, allowing it to award itself ever more emergency powers in the name of security. The junta now has complete control of the nation from this coastal stronghold, and few knowledgeable commenters really believe the promises of a return to democratic elections by next summer.

For our part the western media loves the spectacle. Of the nine million Thais who lived in the capital city almost half were wiped from the face of the earth in the space of just a few hours. Of those not a single man, woman or child made it out alive from the Silom area, the origin of the outbreak, apart from this man who could, conveniently, be played by Hugh Jackman in the movie. When it's inevitably made it will save Hollywood the effort of convincing western audiences that Jackie Chan came from Bangkok.

Paul wobbles back to the table, and as I see him approach I steady our bottles to make sure he won't upset them as he sits. At these prices I can't afford to spill a drop.

"I've only gone and broke the seal," he says, landing heavily in his chair. "Five hours without a piss, and now I'll be up and down every ten minutes."

"Paul, why don't you walk me through what really happened?" My tone is a little impatient. I've been waiting for two hours now while he rambles aimlessly, dropping hints here and there that the story he'd peddled on TV had been as scripted as a soap opera. He'd been the one to reach out to me, not the other way around, and I'm quickly running out of money while he struggles with his conscience.

Paul visibly sobers in front of me. He sighs, reaching for his bound bundle of acrid, hand rolled Indian beedis - the only thing, he says, that blocks out the smell of the undead. He lights one with my fake Zippo and offers the bundle to me. I shake my head and reach for one of my own Marlboro Lights from what must surely be one of the last packs in Thailand.

"OK, here's the truth. It started near the containers of yellow powder. A few of the kids rubbing their eyes, they just went crazy. One cop was helping pour water into the eyes of a little boy, a tiny kid no higher than your waist, and I was staring right at them when the little one launched into him with his fists. The cop slapped him hard and he went down, but by then a few more around him were turning. Poor fucker never stood a chance."

I glance at my notes. "And you were on the flyover at the time, right? What about Ogi?"

Paul visibly flinches at the mention of his wife of four years.

"Yeah, I was well out of it. I was up on the pedestrian walkway above the street, armed with nothing but a fucking camera. Ogi wanted to get in amongst them and get wet, but I was recovering from a broken rib so I didn't want to get jostled. I lost track of her the moment she got down to street level." He stares intently at his beer, once again peeling the label. "Only spotted her once after that."

I wait patiently for Paul to continue, sensing he won't respond well to further prodding.

"Anyway... Once the first couple of guys turned people started to notice. They were right on the edge, near the blockade at Soi Convent, and for a moment even the guys closest to them didn't know what to make of it. They just watched as a group of them launched at the cop. I think they were more surprised than anything else. In Thailand, even drunks don't dare attack cops. That's the quickest way to earn yourself a trip to the hospital." He takes a swig from his beer and lets out a soft, bitter chuckle.

"You want to know why people took a few seconds to get the picture? There was no biting, not at first. We've seen too many zombie movies. We think these things are just teeth on legs, groaning and biting chunks of flesh out of anything with a heartbeat. Zombies – yeah, I know I shouldn't be calling them that – they only bite when they're hungry. That's why most of Bangkok ended up dead rather than turned. Zombies will sooner beat you to death than eat you for lunch."

"I tell you, George Romero should be shot. People were taken by surprise, acting like they were up against movie monsters. I saw a lot of people try to stand their ground with improvised weapons, expecting to give these fuckers a quick crack on the head when they lumbered in. They must have had the fright of their lives when the undead came sprinting, throwing their fists just as hard as real people."

"So how did they attack at first?" I know the answer already. I've seen the snatches of shaky, low-res video a few people around the city managed to upload before the signal dropped out.

"The truth is they're not so different from us. The only real difference is that the little thing most of us have in our heads that makes us stop punching when the other guy goes down is switched off. These fuckers attacked like they were on PCP. Fucking vicious, like a beaten wife who's had enough after years of taking the belt. They used everything they had. Fists. Feet. Fingernails. By the time they were finished with the cop there wasn't much left. Even his eyes were gouged out. Nobody was eating him, though. I guess they weren't peckish."

"Had people started panicking?"

"No, not at first. It only started to go crazy when the group backed away from the cop. That's when people saw it wasn't a regular fight. No way you could make that mistake, not after seeing the body." He stops for a moment as a young family walks by the table, then leans in and continues with a low voice. "You ever seen a riot? A real one, I mean. Not just a protest, but a full on riot? You wouldn't believe it until you saw one. You just can't imagine how much power there is in a crowd. You'd think you could just slip out and get to the edge, but it doesn't work like that. As soon as those things turned towards the crowd, that's when people started to panic. There were enough of the fuckers to block the street, so there was only one way to run: back into the crowd. As soon as that happened, everyone was doomed."

I understand what he means. I remember watching footage of the Hillsborough disaster as a child. 96 people died and almost 800 were injured when crowds at a British soccer stadium crushed forward against crowd control barriers during a cup semi-final. The people at the back of the crowd had no idea they were killing people. There was no way they could have known.

"The problem with Sala Daeng is that you've got a few thousand people packed into a tight space. There's music, laughter, yelling. No way anyone could hear the screaming over the noise. People started to push and shove desperately into the crowd, but what else is new? The crowd just pushed right back and threw their water. It wasn't until someone knocked over the big speakers at the side of the street that the music cut out, and suddenly everyone could hear."

For a moment Paul seems to drift away from me. His eyes lose their focus, and when he continues it's with an odd tone, as if he's reading from a script.

"A scream is... it's a strange noise. You've been hearing them all your life in the movies, but real screams don't sound like that. Actors can't do 'em justice. It's like the difference between a fake laugh and a real one, you know? You can't mistake it. What I heard that day I pray never to hear again. People were screaming so much their voices gave out, but it still wasn't loud enough to drown out the pleading. People were begging for mercy even as their bones broke." He shivers, despite the close heat.

"One girl, some skinny blonde tourist with a long ponytail, panicked and tried to run through the pack to get back to Soi Convent. One of them grabbed her hair, easy as you like, and just tugged it right off her head. I wouldn't have believed it if I hadn't seen it. Fucker just pulled and pulled until her whole scalp just slipped off. Someone must have bit her in the crowd, because she was back on her feet a minute later and joining in the fight for the other side, that ponytail still hanging by a strip of skin halfway down her neck."

I cringe with disgust at the image. I've seen a few walkers with horrific injuries, thankfully on TV rather than up close, and it's all I can do not to wonder how they'd come by them. I thank God I'd never had to watch as someone was turned, or killed.

"Everyone else, of course, pushed right into the crowd. Once the music was gone and people started to hear the screams they all started to shove, but when you've got a few thousand people crowding down half a mile of narrow street it's impossible to get everyone moving as one. Hundreds were trampled. The unlucky ones at the back... well, they were torn to shreds. The really lucky ones, those at the other end of the street, some of them must have managed to get away. It was the people in the middle who lasted the longest. They were squeezed in by the crowds. Some of them managed to stay on their feet. Maybe some even managed to slip away into the shops along the street. That's what I hoped Ogi had done."

"You said you saw her again? In the crowd?"

Paul falls silent for a moment. He stubs out his beedi on the surface of the wooden table, ignoring the ashtray by his bottle.

"Yeah, I... I think so. Seems stupid to say this, but I can't be sure. You know how people say all Asians look alike? Well, it's bullshit. Ogi was Mongolian, looked more Korean than anything else. She definitely didn't look Thai. In that crowd, though, I couldn't have picked her out if she'd been wearing a big sign. Almost everyone had black hair, and I was looking down from above. Everyone was moving too much, squeezing, pushing, pulling. The whole crowd moved like the ocean. Waves of movement pulled people this way and that. Some people tried to scramble over the top, only to fall down and get trampled beneath thousands of feet.

"I think I saw her dress. She was wearing this long, flowing blue floral thing I'd bought for her a couple of weeks earlier in Cambodia. She loved that dress. Said it made her feel like a Parisian, whatever that means. She clambered up on a big plant pot at the side of the street, and I saw that dress for just a second before it vanished. Whether she fell, jumped or was pulled I have no idea. I just know she vanished backwards behind the plants, and that was the last I saw."

"Did you try to call her phone?" I ask.

Paul shoots me a withering look. "Of *course* I tried to fucking call," he snaps. "I called, I sent texts. I called her sister at Bumrungrad Hospital. I called all of our friends. The network was busy every time. Of course that was later. When it all started I had my own problems to deal with. There's another thing I'd like to speak to Romero about. These things are quick as hell. As long as they haven't injured their legs they're just as fast as you and me. It's only later that they slow down, when their joints dry out. When it all kicked off, though... *fuck*, they could move."

"You were chased?"

Paul nods. "I was chased. I made the same stupid 'movie zombie' mistake. I assumed I'd be safe up on the walkway above the street. It never occurred to me that they could climb stairs. I didn't think they could *think*. I was still looking down at the street when I heard a scream to my right, and I turned just in time to see a young Thai woman tip over the railings to escape one of them. She landed with her legs straight, feet first on the street just behind the pack. I almost imagined I could hear her bones snap. I didn't stick around to watch what happened next.

"Everyone started running towards the stairs, heading for the street, but I could see there were too many down there already. A few of the bastards at the back of the crowd had already started to turn away and head back towards the station. Anyway, my decision was made for me."

"How so?"

"The fucker at the top of the stairs locked on to me. Just stared me down from fifty feet away. For a moment – and I know this is stupid – I wondered if I could just slowly back away, no sudden movements, as if I was dealing with one of those crazy soi dogs that run around the city. No chance. The second I twitched he started sprinting at me.

"You know, people who've seen the movies will tell you there's nothing more terrifying than a zombie shambling towards you, groaning all the way like Frankenstein's monster. Film critics say there's something about the slow, unrelenting pace that taps into our primal fear, but I'd like to see one of them come up against a runner. If you're ever unlucky enough to meet a freshly turned fucker you'll know it's bull. I'll see your groaning zombie and raise you a pair of my damp trousers that there's nothing more terrifying than one of them silently sprinting at you full pelt. Fortunately mine hadn't been too quick on his feet when he was alive. He was a little heavy, and he seemed to have trouble running in his sandals. I kicked mine off my feet and shot off down the walkway, towards the MRT station at the end of Silom Road."

I glance down at the hastily sketched map in my pad. "Isn't that where the rest of the infected were heading, too?"

"Yeah, but I had the advantage that I wasn't stopping along the way to rip thousands of people to pieces. The walkway was almost empty, and I soon passed over the crowd. The one chasing me peeled off, too. I risked a look behind me on the straight, and I saw him throw himself over the railing towards the crowd. That's one thing that came in handy. They'll always go for the easiest target. If you can run them in the direction of a limping granny you'll probably get away safe."

Paul notices my expression.

"What, you think you wouldn't? Fuck you, Tom. Trust me, if you ever saw how they kill up close you'd soon change your mind. It's easy to be a hero in theory. In real life... well, you find out pretty fucking quick how brave you really are."

He pauses for a moment, lifts his drink for a swig then reconsiders. "I got back down to street level on the corner of Silom Road and Rama IV. The underground station was right there, but there was no way I'd head down beneath the streets. Unless there was a train waiting for me on the platform... well, I don't want to think would have happened if I'd been trapped down there between the platform barriers. Thousands tried to escape that way, and they're still clearing out the bodies today.

"I ran across the street towards Lumphini Park, the only real green space in the city. Behind me I could hear the traffic go crazy as people were pulled from their cars. As I reached the park gate I turned to see what was happening. I wish I hadn't. It's strange how irrational people become when they're afraid. I saw people jump into cabs that were snarled up in traffic, yelling at the drivers even as the dead came in through the windows. If only they'd kept running they might have gotten away."

"Why do you think they did that? Got in the cabs, I mean," I ask, realizing the pointlessness of the question. Paul looks at me like I'm simple.

"How the fuck should I know? Maybe they thought these things couldn't open doors. They'd be right, for the most part, but a few dozen of them pounding on a window is just as good. A tuk tuk almost managed to get away, jumping onto the sidewalk and cutting through the crowds, living and dead. If only it hadn't hit a hydrant it may have made it, too, but it clipped the steel and bounced off into a shop window. The whole thing went up in flames – those things are death traps at the best of times – and I started running again as the shop began to burn. I can't be sure, but I think that was the start of the fire that tore through all of Silom. I'm damned certain nobody came back to fight it."

"How did you make it to safety? Wasn't your apartment in Thonglor?"

"Yep. It was at least five kilometers as the crow flies, and longer through the streets. I ran all the way once I was in the park. Didn't stop for a breath. Made a few wrong turns, too. Luckily for me, between Lumphini and Thonglor there weren't any train lines. It wasn't until I reached my apartment block that I realized they'd used the trains to overtake me. Some of the wounded from

Silom must have made it up to the platform at Sala Daeng. Some may have even made it all the way to Ratchadamri. I know they didn't turn until they reached the interchange at Siam, 'cause some of them had switched to the Sukhumvit line before it hit them.

"God knows what the other passengers thought. Most of the wounded, I'm guessing, would have just had broken bones. It was only the ones who were bitten that would have turned. Imagine making it through that hell, escaping onto the train only for your friend to turn in the seat beside you. I don't like to think about it. All I know for sure is that the trains were running on auto. They kept making their stops, even after all the passengers were dead. All along Sukhumvit those fuckers poured out at each station. That's why Bangkok got out of control so quickly. The bloody trains. Over the streets and underground those bastards outflanked us all, right out into the suburbs. We never had a chance."

"So why didn't they stop the trains once word got out?"

"Well that's the problem. I don't think word ever really got out. What do you know of the layout of Bangkok? You were only there a few weeks, right? Well, the trains go everywhere, especially since they added the new stations last year. You can barely go anywhere in the center more than 500 meters from the BTS or MRT. The first most people knew about the outbreak was when it came down their street, through their front door, and the trains just kept running, ferrying the bloodthirsty fuckers efficiently around the city.

"That's how they were waiting for me when I got back to Thonglor. An hour of sprinting through back streets, two more hours of creeping around, and when I got back to safety I found they'd beat me to it. The front door of my apartment block was literally at the foot of the stairs to Thonglor BTS station. I was so pleased when I found that place, and now I was cursing it. Convenience goes both ways.

"I approached through the back streets south of Asok and Phrom Phong. Lots of dead ends, lots of alleyways. I heard screams a few times. Doubled back a time or two.

Traffic was non-existent. Bangkok was bumper to bumper most of the time, and the drivers trapped on the main roads would have made handy snacks for the undead. I'd never seen the city so peaceful. Even the air smelled breathable, what with the lack of cars. Shit, hang on."

Paul excuses himself once again, waving for a fresh drink as he walks to the toilet. I light up a Marlboro, take a deep drag and frown at my notes. So far his story bears little resemblance to what had been heard on the news. Paul's official story – the one he'd been spouting on the talk shows every day – was that he'd watched from the flyover as vans sprayed some kind of toxin onto the people on the street below. He'd run down to the street and bravely tried to save as many as he could, killing a terrorist in the process. The body had been recovered by the army, and an investigation of his apartment had found that it had been converted into a lab. The junta had announced that many more such labs had been found across the city, all linked to renters from the Middle East. They'd cited these facts whenever they made a fresh arrest; whenever they confiscated property, deported a foreigner or executed an 'accomplice'.

When Paul returns I ask him why his story had changed.

"Fuck, what does it matter?" he sighs, lighting another foul smelling cigarette. "I liked the idea of being a hero. When I finally made it out of the city and collapsed at the blockade out at Bang Pakong I was too tired to argue. They told me, you see. They told me I had a choice. Either tell the story they wanted me to tell and live like a king, or tell the truth and... they said they'd send me back in."

"So why are you telling me this now? Why did you reach out to me?"

When Paul looks at me it's with eyes much older than his thirty eight years. His voice sounds like it's coming from the bottom of a deep pit far underground, and it cracks a little as he speaks. More than anything, he just sounds tired.

"It doesn't make a difference. They could drop me right back into Silom, and I wouldn't care. Someone should know the truth, before... Anyway, you want to know the worst part? I didn't kill a single zombie. Didn't have it in me. You like to think you'd go all Rambo in that situation. You'd pick up a gun and make a few head shots, at least take a few of them with you before they get you. I just couldn't do it. The moment I got through the security door in my block I cut the power to the keycard reader and pushed a desk in front of the door to wedge it closed. I could hear people banging on it, trying to get in behind me. They were still alive, I know that from the screaming. I just went up to my apartment on the fourth floor, locked the door and waited until the streets were quiet. Three weeks. All I heard were screams. I didn't try to find my wife. I called until my battery died, but the calls would never connect. Maybe she survived. Maybe she was one of the folks screaming at the ground floor, trying to get through the door to safety."

Paul drains his beer in a long gulp, slips another cigarette from his pack and lights it up.

"You always think you'll be a hero, you know?"

He suddenly rises from his chair, throws a handful of cash on the table and walks out of the bar without another word. I wait for half an hour, but he doesn't return.

Paul McQueen was found hanged in his apartment several days after this interview was recorded. He left no suicide note.

****

You have been tried by God, and found wanting. He gave you free will, and He weeps to see how His children have chosen to abuse the precious gift He bestowed upon us. We have strayed from the path the Lord laid out for us. Men lay beside men. Wives no longer serve their husbands. Children no longer respect their parents. Men no longer respect even themselves. They choose to degrade themselves with pornography, and indulge in sinful pleasures that do nothing but destroy the purity the Lord gave them. God is sickened and disgusted by the path we have chosen.

Bangkok was a warning. An ultimatum. A promise. That sinful fleshpot was nothing but a modern day Sodom. The world is purer now its unrighteous denizens have been sent to face the judgment of the Lord, but it was far from unique. Every inch of this planet drowns in sin, and we must now prostrate ourselves before the Lord or be cleansed from this earth.

We offer this message as our final warning. This is your last chance. The human race has one year from today to embrace the Lord God as its sole savior If you fail to repent you will face the final judgment.

We are his divine messengers.

The Sons of the Father

****

That was how it started. A simple message, mailed to media outlets and governments around the world. Everyone from the White House to Fox News to the BBC to Buzzfeed got a copy in their mailbox, and the response from most of them was *"Huh, this crackpot has nice handwriting. How come we don't teach kids cursive anymore?"*

Of *course* nobody took it seriously. Why would they? They must get hundreds of letters every day from bored pranksters and unmedicated psychos, each of them claiming that the world will end next Tuesday, or that 9/11 was a false flag operation orchestrated by Walmart, or that the dog next door had started to speak, and it was craving baby blood and fish tacos. Most of the time those letters go straight in the trash, and most of the time that's exactly where they belong.

It was the same story when the President was fired on in Savannah last summer. When the Secret Service admitted they'd received a threat from the shooter days earlier the media went batshit, accusing them of failing at their most important job. The mania only died down when the President herself came out and released records of the sheer volume of threats she received every day. Thousands of unbalanced assholes scrawl warnings on the back of a napkin. Hundreds of them still have a tight enough grip on reality to figure out how to buy a postage stamp and use a mailbox, and it's up to the Secret Service to trawl through them and determine whether any present a credible threat. It's not an easy job, and sometimes they call it wrong.

In the case of this particular letter... well, absolutely *nobody* thought it was worth a second look. Smart people with years of experience in threat assessment concluded that no terrorist with the capacity to develop sophisticated weapons of chemical warfare would make a threat that looked liked it was written with a quill. They also wouldn't make such a vague, ill defined demand. How could the entire world agree to accept God as its savior? What would happen is everyone got on board but the Swiss? How would you get the OK from every last Masai tribesman? Every herder working high in the Tajik Pamirs? And even if you *could* somehow get everyone to agree, which God are we talking about? The Christian God with the big white beard? Allah? Vishnu? Bill Murray?

No, none of this fit the profile of a legitimate threat. It was just a bad, weird joke from some addled crackpot who didn't understand the meaning of 'too soon', and it was filed away with the rest of them.

The letter was reported, of course, simply because it went everywhere. Thousands of them were mailed out, each one exquisitely handwritten, and that was enough to make a few reporters sit up and take notice. They didn't believe the warning but they thought it was interesting that someone had clearly gone to a lot of effort to scare the shit out of people. Interesting enough to report it in the *And finally...* segment of the nightly news, anyway.

And then it was forgotten almost as soon as it was mentioned. The President was gearing up for a tough re-election campaign. The Saudis were threatening to flood the market and push oil below $15 a barrel again. There was a mass shooting at Disney World. We all had bigger things to worry about than some random crackpot with excellent penmanship.

Hell, even the fall of Bangkok was quickly pushed aside by more urgent news. Sure, millions of people had died, but it happened on the other side of the world and it happened to people who weren't Americans. Bangkok might as well be on Mars for all it mattered to folks from Tulsa.

Even *I* let it slip to the back of my mind, and it meant more to me than most. In the months following my interview with Paul McQueen I couldn't sleep through the night without waking in a sheen of cold sweat, my twisted sheets stuck to my skin and the image of Paul's sunken, haunted eyes burned into my mind like the afterglow from a bright light. I imagined I could smell the acrid smoke of his disgusting Indian cigarettes as I woke, their odor masking the stench of decaying flesh. The nightmares followed me all the way back home where I took a room in a Brooklyn apartment owned by Jim Bryson, an old high school buddy who'd made it big in apps.

This shit *scared* me. I became convinced that Paul hadn't been crazy. The story he told me was entirely true, I was sure of it. The western world was certain that the culprits were Muslim jihadists - a comfortable narrative that fit our preconceptions and helped justify our disastrous ground campaign in Syria - but I knew better.

Paul had described the terrorists as western with shaved heads, and one of the few things anyone had been able to learn about the Sons of the Father was that - before they seemed to vanish from the face of the earth a decade ago - they'd been a small, radical offshoot of the Baptists, almost identical in their beliefs to the crazy bastards at the Westboro Church, only these guys had a weird belief that it was immodest for body hair to be exposed. They shaved every last strand down to the skin.

For months I tried to get people interested in the story. I ran a failed Kickstarter campaign to raise money for a documentary on Bangkok and the threat of the Sons. I self published a book that moved fewer than a hundred free copies. I spent endless hours on conspiracy forums, trying to get someone - *anyone* - to pay attention to the idea that the warning might be legit, but even the tinfoil hat brigade couldn't be distracted from the latest GMO scandal long enough to give me more than a dismissive *'cool story, bro.'* It was frustrating, to say the least.

And then... then I met a woman, a cute barista who worked at my local coffee place. She had dimples in her cheeks. She stole good coffee beans from work for me. She warmed her feet by squeezing them between my thighs as we sat curled up on the couch watching Daredevil on Netflix. I don't want to say I fell head over heels - there have been too many women over the years to kid myself that this one might be *the* one - but it was *nice*. It was comfortable and safe, and that's exactly what I needed.

Suddenly it seemed a little pointless to obsess about my theory. It seemed crazy to sit at my laptop until 3AM, raving on forums while Kate was waiting for me to keep her warm in bed. I managed to convince myself that I'd just gone a little crazy. Meeting Paul just days before he took his own life had sent me off the deep end, and Kate was helping pull me back to dry land.

Gradually, day by day, week by week, I spent less time trying to convince people that the world was going to end and more time enjoying the world I had now. Kate made me forget it all. She made me forget my plan to leave the city for a shack out in the woods. She made me set aside my plan to learn how to shoot, trap game, filter water and dress a wound with my eyes closed. She made me forget everything but those cute little dimples that appeared whenever she smiled.

Looking back, this was a pretty fucking huge mistake.

Dimples aren't worth shit at the end of the world.

****

April 7th, 2019

It's the rain that wakes me. Thick, heavy
drops, bouncing like ball bearings against the
window above the bed. It sounds like it's
gusting outside, pushing the rain in sheets so
it falls unevenly on the glass... *tap, tap, tap,
tap, taptaptaptap, tap, tap, tap, tap,* like a
sudden flurry of applause.

I crack open one eye and crane my neck to
the old fashioned alarm clock on the bedside
table, a black cast iron beast with a scrap of
sponge squeezed beneath the bell to muffle
the alarm. It's just after eleven in the
morning. I roll on my back and stretch,
grinning to myself as I remember it's
Saturday. Nothing to do today but watch TV
in my underwear until Kate gets home from
work. Maybe I'll cook. Nah. Maybe I'll just
order pizza. It feels like a pizza day.

taptaptaptaptaptap.

I feel something wet and cold splash against
my cheek, and I look up at the window to
find it's cracked open a few inches. With

each gust a little spray finds its way through the gap to my bed. It's kinda nice. Brooklyn has been unseasonably warm these past few days, and we don't have any AC in this old place. It's nice to be woken by a cool shower and that strangely pleasant smell of city rain. Musty and damp, but oddly refreshing.

I reach out to hunt for the remote buried somewhere in the sheets on Kate's side of the bed. I know it's in here somewhere. Kate always watches dumb cartoons late into the night, and she usually falls asleep clutching the remote like a security blanket. I fish around blindly for a minute before finding it hidden beneath her pillow, then point it in the direction of the TV and mash at random buttons until the screen flickers to life.

"— new information at this time, but we'll stay on the air and keep you updated as long as we can. We're hearing... We're... Hold on, please, I have my producer in my ear..."

I squint at the TV, confused. The little orange network logo in the corner of the screen tells me I'm tuned to Nickelodeon, but there's a news anchor on screen, some middle aged silver haired guy. I want to say

Anderson Cooper, but I'm not sure. Skinny dude, looks like a prematurely gray college senior.

"... OK... Uh huh..." He presses his ear as he speaks, listening to someone through an earpiece. He looks flustered, his face shiny and flushed. "OK, I'm being told that the President is preparing to address the nation. We'll take you live to the White House just as soon as—" The image switches to the presidential seal without warning, cutting the anchor off mid-sentence.

I sit bolt upright, suddenly fully awake. *What the fuck is going on?* The seal stays on screen for ten seconds. Fifteen. Twenty. I start to wonder if there's been some sort of technical problem, or maybe my signal has frozen. I quickly flip through the channels to see what else is showing, but each channel shows the exact same seal, like every frequency has been hijacked.

tap, tap, TAP, taptaptaptap.

The seal finally vanishes, replaced by a color pattern, and a few seconds later the image flickers to what looks like the Oval Office.

The ornately carved Resolute desk fills much of the screen, but there's nobody in the seat behind it.

A few moments of silence, and then an irritated voice calls out off camera. "No makeup, Karl. Look, just... oh, for the love of God, just give it to me."

An urgent voice whispers, "We're live, ma'am."

The room falls silent for a moment, then comes the rustling sound of a mic being attached to clothing, and a few seconds later the President appears on screen and lowers herself behind the desk. She looks awful, like she's aged ten years overnight. Behind the desk she looks much smaller than the larger than life ballbuster we elected three years ago. She looks... well, she looks like a little old lady. It's hard to imagine that this is a woman about to embark on a year long high energy re-election campaign. She looks like she should have been buried yesterday.

"My fellow Americans," she begins, her voice hoarse and rasping, "it pains me deeply to break this news, but I must report that our great nation is under attack. A little more than five hours ago law enforcement in New York City and here in Washington D.C. began to report acts of unexplained large scale rioting and civil disobedience. Local authorities were quickly overwhelmed, and following the advice of the Pentagon, the Secretary of Defense and my Joint Chiefs of Staff I dispatched units of the National Guard to assist in operations to secure these cities. The current status of these units is unknown."

She looks as if her attention is distracted by someone off-camera. I hear the sound of a door creak open, and quiet but insistent voices in the background. The President scowls and shakes her head. She turns back to the camera.

"We don't yet know if these events are related to last year's attack on Bangkok. I cannot currently give you the exact details of the situation, or of any ongoing operations undertaken by our military and civilian forces, but you can rest assured that the brave men and women of our armed forces, police force and fire department are working tirelessly to bring this situation under control and restore peace."

She keeps her eyes trained on the camera, but raises a warning hand to someone off screen.

"As of this moment I am declaring a national state of emergency. All air, rail and sea transport has been grounded until further notice. Our national borders have been closed, and stock market trading has been suspended. I urge citizens to follow any and all directions given by the authorities, and I implore you all to keep— what? *No*! I'm not finished."

These last words are angry and directed off-camera. Moments later the view is blocked by a posse of black-suited Secret Service agents who hustle the President to her feet, loudly protesting, and whisk her quickly from the room. I can barely make out anything in the confusion, but I think I hear one of the agents say something like "They've breached the perimeter." There's an edge of panic in his voice.

taptaptaptaptaptap, tap, tap, tap.

In the confusion someone must have knocked the camera. The image wheels away from the desk, blurring until it suddenly comes to rest pointing at a desk leg and the plush blue carpet. For a few seconds the camera struggles to find focus, alternating between the desk and a random point on the floor while sounds of movement come from off-screen. The final words I hear are "Eagle moving" before the image suddenly cuts back to the anchor, who looks like he wasn't expecting the camera to be on him. He's staring off-screen at a monitor, and it takes a few seconds for him to realize he's live. He hurriedly drops something he's holding to the ground, but from the curl of smoke hanging in the air it's clear he was smoking in the newsroom.

"Umm... We'll... Yeah, OK, we'll try to get the White House back as soon as possible. In the meantime I'd like to repeat our earlier message. If your area is affected, please remain in your home. Do not attempt to leave. If you are at your place of work, do not attempt to return home. Do not attempt to..." He looks off screen. "Jack, I'm not fucking telling people to..." He sighs, exasperated. "OK, OK. Do not attempt to reach loved ones. Lock all doors and windows, and move to the most secure room in your building. Gather any food you have and fill as many containers as you can find with water, and prepare as best you can for possible power outages.

"If your area is *not* currently affected you should tune your set to local broadcasts for details of evacuation plans. Jack, do we have the frequency? The... umm, the emergency... OK, I'm being told that the emergency alert system will soon be broadcasting local information across all radio frequencies, including digital bands. We understand that authorities are currently establishing safe zones on the outskirts of several cities with sufficient food, power and fresh water to support all those who wish to —"

The signal suddenly drops out, leaving the room cast in the blue glow from the menu screen, and eerily silent but for the rain drumming against the window.

tap, tap, tap, tap, tap.

My mind is running a mile a minute. I have no way of knowing for sure, but I can only assume that my worst nightmare has come true. The deadline given by the Sons of the Father was a little more than a week ago. That day came and went like any other, and it was so far from my mind that I barely registered my relief when the sun set without incident. Now it seems like I was right all along. The shit just hit the fan a little later than scheduled.

Taptaptaptap.

I pull myself to my feet, almost in a trance. None of this seems real. *Did the President say New York? Jesus. Am I safe? Is Kate safe? Is this really* - I almost laugh out loud at the insane thought - *is this really a fucking zombie outbreak?*

I suddenly feel like I'm suffocating. I've never had a panic attack, but this sure feels like one. I feel like the walls are closing in, and the air feels like it's been drained of its oxygen. I stagger over to the window and yank it fully open, stick my head out and inhale a lungful of fresh, cool air.

Tap, tap, taptaptap.

The street outside my window is empty of traffic, but that's not out of the ordinary since this is a dead end road. It's usually pretty quiet out there. Something is niggling at me, though, tickling at the back of my mind. There's something obvious that I really should have already noticed, but my mind doesn't seem to want to connect the dots. *What are you missing, Tom? Think!*

I stare out at the street and try to imagine what's going on in the city. I wonder where Kate might be. Her coffee shop is just a few streets over. Surely she'd try to come back here when she heard the—

My mind suddenly clears, and I realize what my subconscious is yelling at me to notice.

tap, tap, taptaptaptap, tap, tap.

The sound of raindrops, still bouncing off the window like ball bearings.

Only it's not rain. The rain has stopped.

tap, tap... tap.

That's the sound of gunfire.

And it's close.

****

"Bryson! Jim, are you home?"

My voice echoes through the halls, but it's not met with an answer. I didn't really expect one. Bryson usually spends Friday night with one of the many women in Manhattan who are more than happy to push their soft toys to the floor for a good looking guy with a wallet bursting at the seams. Right now he's probably sleeping off a champagne hangover in some NYU student dorm.

I stalk down the hallway aimlessly, still struggling to get my head around the enormity of what's going on. I lean back against the wall and take a deep breath, trying to focus and center myself, then I slap my forehead in disbelief that I haven't thought to check my damned phone yet.

I run back to my room, dive on the bed and fish my iPhone from beneath the duvet. 17% battery. Three bars.

Jesus, a dozen missed calls, and almost as many texts. I had the damned thing set to silent.

"*Oh fuck oh fuck oh fuck* please be OK, Kate. Please God, let her be OK."

I tap the screen and bring up the log. Most of the calls are from Kate, with a couple from unknown numbers. I tap onto the texts and my blood runs cold as I read them.

Heading to work babe. Korean BBQ tonight?

****

Cn u call me? Hearing weird stuff from customers.

****

Babe, pick up.

****

DUCKING PICK UP!

****

Jesus, turn on the news! Have you seen what's happening on the bridge? I'm coming home. Stay there!

****

PLEASE let me know you're safe. In the antique place. People trying to get in. Scared.

****

Hefl us were flicking stuck

****

Tom I need to turn off my phone they can. Hear me. Don't call just get out I love you so much.

****

The phone slips from my fingers onto the bed, and I feel the crushing weight of guilt squeeze at my chest. I was sleeping soundly while Kate was going through all of this, terrified. The first text was sent three hours ago, at 8AM when she was just arriving at work. I scroll to the final message, and my heart leaps into my throat when I see it was sent twenty minutes ago, just minutes before I woke up.

OK, what the fuck do you do now, Tom?
Think! Take a breath and just fucking
THINK!

"OK," I say out loud, trying to calm myself with my own voice. "She's three blocks from here. Let's say five minutes on foot. Move slowly. Look around the corners. Keep to cover. OK, weapon. Weapon, weapon, weapon."

As I tug on my clothes I scan the room for something suitable, thinking back to what Paul McQueen had said when he described the Bangkok attack. He said people tried to fight as if they were up against slow, lumbering movie monsters. They thought they could be taken out with a quick blow to the head, but the things moved too fast for the survivors to properly defend themselves.

At least I have the benefit of a minute or two to catch my breath and think. Those poor bastards in Bangkok had only seconds to react, and they were limited to whatever they had to hand. Plastic water guns and buckets, mostly. I'm sure I can find something a little more suitable.

My eyes settle on the aluminum baseball bat poking out from beneath my bed. I'd give my right arm for a gun and a full box of ammo, but beggars can't be choosy. I tug it out and swing it a few times, accustoming myself to the weight and balance.

I know it's not an ideal weapon. It feels much too light to take down an adult, but it might just do the job until I can get my hands on a gun. I figure I'll do my best to stay away from anything moving, and if I'm forced into a confrontation I'll go in at a dead sprint and just swing away at anyone coming at me. I won't go for a head shot, but I'll just try to get them the fuck out of my way and tear ass out of there.

I'm about to walk out of the room when an image flashes into my mind, of Brad Pitt in that zombie movie. He taped magazines to his arms as makeshift gauntlets, protecting them against bites. I don't have any tape in the house - I shake my head in disgust at my lack of even the most basic preparation - but I might be able to give myself similar protection. I drop to my knees and reach blindly under the bed, probing with my fingers until I find what I'm searching for.

It's my old high school baseball mitt. Thick, stiff, biteproof leather. This thing has been sitting under the bed so long the leather has dried out and turned brittle, but there's no way in hell anyone could bite through it. On the off chance an attacker decides he's hungry I want to be able to hold him off with something other than a handful of tasty, chewable fingers.

I tug the mitt down over my left hand, tap the bat against my leg and scan the room, looking for anything else that might be useful. Once again I curse myself for neglecting to prepare for this shit. I can't believe I allowed myself to become so fucking complacent. I don't even have a basic bug out bag. No real weapons. No water filter. Not even a bag of trail mix to keep me going. What the fuck was I thinking? I had such big plans. I was going to become a *real* man, one of those guys who takes the apocalypse in his stride. I wanted to be Daryl from The Walking Dead, a badass tracker with a crossbow slung across his back. Right now I wouldn't even make it to the end of the first episode.

OK, time to go, Tom. Get out of your damned head. Be careful. Pay attention. Don't do anything dumb.

I turn out of the room and walk down the hall, trailing the bat behind me across the wooden floor. I reach the front door of the apartment, grip the doorknob, take a deep breath and...

"*Jesus*, Tom," I sigh, slapping my mitt against my forehead in disbelief at my own stupidity. "Put on some fucking shoes, you moron."

****

Distant gunfire echoes through the otherwise silent street. It sounds like it's coming from all directions, shifting with the wind. Most of it sounds like it's way off, but every dozen steps I flinch as a shot rings out dangerously close.

I pause at the end of the street, peering timidly around the corner to the main road. Empty. Silent. About half a block away a Prius sits in the middle of the road facing in my direction, blocking the street between both banks of parked cars. The front driver's door hangs open, but there's nobody to be seen.

I lean back against the wall and take a mental inventory to calm myself. I look down at my feet, starting from the ground up. A pair of thick, scuffed Alden boots, a hangover from the days I liked to pretend I was Indiana Jones while I tooled around the Mongolian countryside. Heavyweight jeans, the thickest I own. I've no idea if they'll help if some infected fucker tries to take a bite out of me, but it won't make me an easy meal.

I move further up. Two plain gray t-shirts, layered one over the other in case I need spare cotton for... I don't know, bandages? Might come in handy. Onto my coat, a vintage Belstaff Trialmaster motorcycle jacket. I'm pleased with this one. The thick waxed cotton might offer my some bite protection, but the really useful thing is the detachable belt. Could come in handy as a tourniquet, if it comes to it.

I pat my pockets. Cigarettes, because fuck it. If the world is about to end at least I don't have to worry about cancer any more. Two disposable lighters, and a freshly filled Zippo that still stinks of lighter fluid.

In my right jeans pockets I feel the outline of my house key, looped to a tiny little three inch Victorinox pen knife with a blade so blunt it'd struggle to open a letter, and in my left my iPhone, complete with documentary evidence that I'm just the shittiest of shitty boyfriends, sleeping off too many Friday night beers while my girlfriend pleaded for help.

I've been thinking about that final message since I saw it, and even now at the worst possible time I hear it repeating over and over in my head. *I love you so much.* Beneath the fear and dread twisting my hungover stomach I feel the unpleasant grip of... guilt, I guess? Shame? I don't know what it is, exactly, but a pretty big part of me wants to turn around and run in the opposite direction.

I don't love Kate. I don't know how else to put it. I just don't love her, and I never said I did. I like her a whole bunch. I love *spending time* with her - that old dodge - but I'm not *in* love with her. It was probably a bad idea to ask her to move in with me, but it just felt right at the time. It felt like the adult thing to do, and a good way to rescue myself from the pit I'd fallen down.

And now I'm walking through Brooklyn with a flimsy aluminum baseball bat trying to rescue her, because again that's the grown up thing to do. It's the thing Paul McQueen *didn't* do, and even with my world collapsing around me I don't want anyone to judge me the way I judged him. I don't want people to think I'm a coward who'd abandon his girlfriend. I'm putting myself in harm's way *because I don't want people to think less of me.*

Jesus, I'm fucked up.

I push the thought from my head, take a deep breath, heft the baseball bat so I can grip it in the middle, and turn into the street. I stick close to the walls on the south side of the road, the red brick still wet from the rain. The sound of my jacket scraping against the rough surface sounds deafening in the eerie silence. I take a step away, terrified that a thousand killers might hear me and come flooding around the corner.

Nothing comes.

Where is everybody?

The Prius is just a few dozen feet away now, and I stop behind the cover of a parked Lincoln to cautiously check it out. It's not crashed. It just looks abandoned, like the driver had to get out of there in a hurry, and I wonder if he might have left the key in the ignition. The roads look clear enough, and I figure the quiet electric motor might make it a perfect stealthy getaway vehicle once I find Kate.

I decide to risk stepping out into the open. The gunfire sounds like it's all far away now. Whoever was shooting nearby a minute ago seems to have stopped. I step out from behind the Lincoln and slowly, carefully make my way towards the Prius, creeping from car to car, my head low.

It's just a few feet from me now. I cross the street stealthily and slowly lower myself to the ground to check out the space beneath the car. All clear. I stand up and walk to the door, but the moment I reach out and touch the frame I hear a sound that makes my blood freeze in my veins.

Breathing. Slow, wet, rasping breath, like the sucking sound made by the gross little spit vacuum at the dentist.

And it's coming from inside the car.

She comes out of nowhere, launching herself from the back seat towards the dashboard. It all happens too fast to take anything in, but I fall back onto my ass and kick out reflexively, randomly, like a toddler who doesn't want his diaper changed. I don't even realize my foot has connected with the door until I see it slam shut in her face just as she throws herself towards me. Her head bounces against the window with a sickening *thunk* as the door slams shut.

My ears are ringing and spots flash in front of my eyes, and it takes a few seconds before I realize the crazed, gulping sobs I hear are coming from me. I swallow hard and force myself to take a slow, shuddering breath. *Control yourself, Tom. Stop fucking panicking.*

I sit there for a moment, my foot pressed against the door just long enough to be sure that it's firmly closed, then push myself from the ground and look in the car.

She's just a kid. Can't be more than ten years old. A cute, chubby little blonde thing, her long hair plaited like the princess from Frozen. She doesn't look like there's anything wrong with her. I can't see any visible wounds from here, apart from the bright red trickle of blood rolling down her forehead from the wound that opened up when she hit the window. She doesn't even have that glazed, milky contact lens look these things always have in the movies. She just looks like a little girl. Snarling and crazed, but a little girl all the same. If I didn't know better I'd assume she was just a normal kid throwing a violent tantrum.

I can't help but feel sorry for her as I watch her watching me. Now the door is closed and I lock eyes with her she holds still, meeting my gaze like a dog asserting its dominance. She looks like she's gone into low power mode, like she's waiting for the next stimulus to trigger an attack.

Not for the first time I wish the Thais hadn't been so fucking stubborn and pigheaded in the wake of their attack. The junta burned most of the bodies, and nobody knows what happened to the few walkers still on their feet after the military firebombed the remains of Bangkok. The Thais refused to share much of what they'd learned about these things. They insisted it was an internal matter, and as General Kantawat descended deeper into paranoid madness the government stopped even talking with the wider world.

God, the things we could have learned if they'd just shared with us. We might have been able to stop this. We might have found a vaccine. We might even have found a way to cure it. This cute, chubby little girl might have been saved with a simple injection, but instead she's staring into my eyes through the glass, a glob of bloody pink spit drooling down her chin as she snarls. She's done. Gone. If her parents are still alive they'll never see their daughter again.

I'm not sure they'd even *want* to see her. Not like this. I don't know her, and even *I* can hardly bear to look into those eyes and see nothing I recognize as human looking back at me. She's just an animal now. This sweet little kid probably woke up early this morning to catch some cartoons while she munched on Cheerios, and now she's nothing but a vehicle for violence. I know she'd try to kill me if I gave her an inch. She'd sink her teeth into my flesh and tear away a chunk if I opened the door right now.

I feel hot tears stream down my cheeks. I know the smart thing to do would be to get the fuck out of here before this little monster breaks through the window or figures out the door handle. If she manages to get out of her prison I'd better be far away.

A small part of me, though, whispers that I should free her from this hell. I should crack open the door just enough to slide my bat through the gap and give her a few sharp jabs in the face with the handle until her brain switches off. After all, what kind of a life does this pathetic little thing have to look forward to? Her best case scenario is that she escapes the car and goes on to kill and eat a bunch of people. It's not like she can look forward to college. She'll never have an awkward first date. She'll never make out with some kid from the football team in the back row of a theater. She's lost. Whatever made her human has gone, and the kind thing to do would be to end her suffering.

Common sense kicks in before I let myself reach out for the door handle. I have no clue how strong these things are. My only experience of them is a second hand story from an old friend who, to be fair, wasn't of sound mind when I last spoke to him. I don't know what this girl is capable of. Maybe she could spit the infection at me. Hell, maybe it's airborne. Maybe just opening the door again would be enough for it to work its way into my system and turn me into one of these mindless monsters. It may be too late already, for all I know. It might already be in my blood. The countdown may have already begun.

In any case, I have no idea if I could even bring myself to kill her. They make it look easy in the movies. A quick swing of the bat and the thing goes down, threat neutralized, but a nasty little thought in the back of my mind tells me that the reality wouldn't be quite so PG13. I'm guessing the reality is much, much messier, and the kind of thing that would lead to years of therapy. I'd pound away with the heel of the bat until this sweet little kid's face caved in. She'd probably keep snarling as I turned her head into jelly, and she wouldn't stop until I finally drove enough shards of shattered skull into her brain to turn the fucking thing off. I don't know if I have the will to do that. Or the strength, for that matter. I haven't so much as thrown a punch in ten years, and who knows how much force it would take to kill her?

I turn away from the car before I can dwell on it any longer, and jump with shock as the little girl begins to pound her head hard against the glass. My movement set her off again, and now she's once again crazed. With each dull thump against the window the wound in her forehead spreads open wider, and the glass quickly smears with so much blood it looks like she's hiding behind a stained glass window.

I can't watch any longer. It doesn't look like she has the strength to break through, but I can't bear to see her destroy herself.

I hurry away from the car, moving on in the direction of the antique store where I hope - where I *need* - to find Kate. As I walk I can't help but wonder what it's like to be one of those things. Is that little girl still in there somewhere, trapped in the back of a mind now controlled by a monster? Is she watching what's happening to her through eyes she can't control, watching her own limbs move against her will, like a puppet?

Can she feel pain? Is she afraid? Does she miss her parents?

I shake my head to evict such thoughts, and remind myself that the more I dwell on questions like this the more likely it becomes that I'll get to learn the answers first hand. I need to be vigilant. I can't walk around in a daze, asking myself pointless questions while the world goes to shit. Survival is all that matters right now. Philosophy can take a number.

I reach another intersection, the last before the commercial block with Kate's coffee shop at its center After reading her texts I expect the antique store across the street from her place to be swarming with the infected, and I feel my heart thump madly in my chest as I creep towards the corner.

I crouch down low and hold my breath before I poke my head around the wall, as if the things could hear my breathing at fifty paces. I hardly dare look. I know what I see around the corner will tell me if she's dead, and... well, I really don't want to know. I don't want to replace the terrifying hope of *maybe* with the crushing, leaden finality of *no*.

I force myself to look. With the handle of the bat gripped tight in my fist I creep forward to the corner of the intersection and slowly poke my head out, peering down the road.

Nothing. No one.

The street looks like it would on any other quiet Saturday morning. No bodies. The road is free of traffic. A couple of cars are parked illegally in the no stopping zone like always, a calculated risk while the drivers run in to grab a coffee to go. My eyes scan the street looking for signs of movement but it's quiet as the grave. The front door of the old used bookstore is wide open, as is the door of the Whole Foods next door. Kate's coffee shop still has tables sat outside, with paper cups resting there as if the customers have all stepped inside to take a piss.

I walk out into the street, a little more confident now, and hurry along the row of parked cars until I reach the antique store directly opposite the coffee shop. As I approach it my pace slows, and I come to a halt out front with a sinking feeling in my heart.

The big bay window has been shattered from the outside. In the dim, dusty interior I can see shards of glass sprayed across the ground. I try the door, but it only opens a couple of inches before hitting up against some sort of heavy object.

Slowly, carefully I climb into the store through the broken window, watching out for the glittering shards still clinging to the frame, and I immediately see what happened. A heavy armoire has been pushed up against the door to form a blockade. It looks like it worked, but there was nothing large enough to block the windows.

I feel a lump rise in my throat as I imagine hordes of snarling, wailing creatures flooding in through the shattered window like water, filling every inch of the space inside and overwhelming anyone hiding within. It must have been terrifying.

I choke down a desperate sob and lean against the armoire, fishing my phone from my jacket pocket. There's no harm in trying to call now. Whatever was looking for Kate surely found her, but I don't want to give up that last scrap of hope that she might answer and tell me that she's fine. That she's sitting pretty in a chopper that arrived at the last minute to carry her to safety, and she's on her way to a safe zone outside the city. That I don't have to feel this *guilt*.

I scroll to Kate's name, hover over it for a moment with my thumb, then bite the bullet and press the screen. I don't really expect the call to connect. I have two bars, but I don't know what that really means. I've no idea if the cell network is even still working. I've -

I hear a sound. Faint, right on the edge of my hearing.

It sounds like a phone.

"Tom?" A tinny voice calls out, too loud, and I press the phone to my ear to take it out of loudspeaker mode. "Tom, is that you?"

"Kate!" I cry, too shocked and ecstatic to keep my voice down. "Oh my God, I thought you were dead!"

"Tom, can you hear me? I can't hear you."

In the background I can hear a male voice whisper, "It sounds like it's going away. We have to move *now*."

"Kate, can you hear me?" I hear the desperation in my own voice. "Please, tell me where you—"

She speaks over me. "I don't know if you're there, but I'm stuck in the antique store across the street from work. One of them was trying to get through the door, but we think it just left. We're gonna make a break for it, OK? I'm gonna try to get home." I hear her voice waver with emotion. "Oh, please tell me you can hear me, Tom... I love you."

"I love you," I whisper, but the call has already cut out. I don't know why I said it. It just seemed like the right thing to do. *Jesus*, I'm an idiot.

I slip the phone back in my pocket, then freeze as my brain finally catches up with what the call means. Kate is here somewhere, still in the store. Still alive.

And one of *them* is in here with us. Not trapped behind a door. Out. Free. *Roaming*.

I hear a loud thump from somewhere in the back of the store and I feel my grip tighten on the bat. Another thump. Whatever it is, it's coming closer. Another, even closer this time, as if a drunk guy is stumbling his way towards me. The bat suddenly feels far too light and flimsy.

It occurs to me that it was my own voice that drew the thing away from Kate. It heard me, and now it's come to hunt me down. The hairs on the back of my neck stand on end, and the grip of the bat feels slippery in my sweat drenched hand.

The thing finally appears, limping slowly through the door to the back room. I pull back against the wall into the shadow of a large grandfather clock, trying to blend into the shadows as best I can.

It's an old man, maybe late sixties. Neat gray hair, and a fussy little silver beard that looks like it received loving attention each morning. As he emerges from the behind the counter I see why he's limping. He has an enormous shard of glass embedded in his bony thigh, jutting forward about six inches and buried so deep that it barely wobbles as he walks.

He doesn't seem to notice the pain, even as he bumps against a low table and presses the shard deeper into his thigh. His cream trousers are soaked crimson down one leg. His knuckles are bruised and bloody.

I hold my breath as he slowly approaches, wishing the grandfather clock was just a little bigger. In the silence all I can hear is the slow drag of feet and soft, rasping breath from the creature. He seems to be moving away towards the window, and I pray he'll climb through.

He reaches the glass and pauses, as if his slow, broken mind is processing the best way to negotiate the window frame. I can almost see his mind tick over like an idling engine, and once again I wonder what's going on in there.

He seems to come to a decision. Slowly - too slowly for my bursting lungs - he lifts his bad leg clumsily over the lip of the window. He moves to set his foot down in the street, and—

—And the minute hand of the grandfather clock beside me ticks over, breaking the cloying silence with a loud, dull *tock*.

The creature whips his head towards me and locks eyes with mine. I freeze in place, shocked by the cold, mindless hatred in those eyes, and stifle a cry as he pulls back into the store and suddenly runs - *sprints* - towards me with terrifying speed.

I know I don't have the space to swing the bat. I don't have the time to think straight, but I instinctively know I'll still be on the back swing by the time he's on me. There's only one thing I can do. As he barrels towards me I thrust out the heel of my left hand, still clad in the heavy leather mitt, and drive it forward and up into the man's chin, my arm locked at the elbow. I watch in slow motion as he opens his mouth to bite, and I cringe as my blow forces his mouth shut, catching his tongue between his teeth and cleanly severing the tip. I imagine I can feel the tiny chunk of wet flesh spit against the palm of my hand as the man falls backwards, stunned.

Now I'm working on autopilot. No conscious thought passes through my mind as I lift the bat and step forward to take my first heavy overarm swing. I swing like I'm chopping wood, bringing the aluminum rod over my head and down hard onto the man's forehead. He seems to react with anger rather than pain, snapping at me and trying to lift himself back to his feet, but I move too quickly for him. I swing again, sending him back to the ground with a fresh gash in his cheek, and again. Again. Repeating, over and over, his face caving in deeper with each blow until he isn't recognizable as a man any more. Now he's just a mass of swollen flesh, as misshapen as a Picasso portrait, one cheek sunken and caved, the other exposed, raised bone.

I keep swinging long after he's stopped struggling to stand. Long after he's stopped moaning. I swing until I can't tell the difference between head and floor. Until he's just a body cut off at the wrinkled, sinewy neck, ending in a glistening pink and white jellied mass of flesh and bone.

"Tom!" A voice cries out to my left.

I swing the bat toward the sound instinctively, my arms barely connected to my mind, and the aluminum crashes against the dark wood of the grandfather clock.

"Tom, *stop*!"

The voice finally breaks though. The red mist starts to fade, and I feel myself regaining control. I blink a few times and try to make sense of what I'm seeing.

It's Kate, her face just inches from the end of the dented, bloody bat. She looks down at the mess twitching at my feet then back up at me, and slowly, carefully reaches out to pull the bloodied bat from my hand.

"I think you got him, babe."

****

I stare at my reflection in the curved, mirrored surface of the cappuccino machine, and I barely recognize the face looking back at me. It's the same face I was wearing when I visited the coffee shop yesterday, but now a thin crust of brown blood dries quickly on my cheeks. My hair is matted, clumped together and stuck to my forehead. I reach up and run my fingers through it then stare dumbly at my stained hand. The hand I just used to murder a fellow human being.

I flinch when I feel Kate's hand on my shoulder, then look down and see that my clothes didn't escape the blood spray. I look like I've spent my morning painting a room red.

"Don't touch me!" I yell, shying away from Kate's hand.

She steps back in surprise. "What? Why?"

I tug my jacket off and drop it to the ground. "Look at your hand. I'm covered in this shit. Here, give me your hands." I pull her to the basin by the register and twist open the faucet with my elbow. "We have to keep ourselves clean. Who knows how this thing spreads? Maybe a single drop of blood in your eyes or mouth is enough to fuck you up. We can't take any risks until we know what's going on, OK?"

I wait for Kate to clean herself off, then dunk my head under the tap with my eyes closed and my lips pressed shut. After a minute I risk cracking open one eye, and I see the water swirling down the drain is running clear.

Next comes my jacket. I grab a towel from the stack by the basin, soak it wet then wipe down the waxed cotton until the worst of the blood seems to be gone. Death by contaminated jacket would be a really dumb way to check out.

Kate watches me as I dry myself off. She reaches her hand to her mouth and moves to chew her thumbnail, a nervous habit, but catches herself in time and forces her hand to her side. "Shit, this is really happening, isn't it?" she says, with fear in her voice. "All that stuff you used to say about Bangkok. This is it, right? Sons of the whatever, zombie plague, end of the world shit. It was all true?"

I nod solemnly.

"Well... *damn*." She lowers herself to a stool by the counter. "I always just assumed you were a little weird when you talked about that stuff. You know, like someone who thinks they faked the moon landings. It never occurred to me that you might actually be right."

I manage a hollow laugh. "Well thanks, honey. It's nice to know I can always count on you for support."

"Oh, you know what I mean. It's just... Jesus, I mean this is really *it*. No more coffee shop. No more McDonalds breakfast. No more... oh shit, no more *Game of Thrones*."

She sees my expression.

"Come on, don't look at me like that. I just mean... you know, it's *over*. All that day to day shit we took for granted, it's *done*."

"Yeah, pretty much," I reply, shrugging my jacket back over my shoulders. "I just wish I'd done more to prepare for it. I don't have a plan. I have no clue where we go from here, Kate. Shit, I don't even have a damned gun. How am I gonna protect us?"

Kate smiles for the first time. "Oh, I don't know. You were pretty good with that bat."

I look down at the bloodied aluminum bat resting on the counter. "I guess. It won't last long, though. It's already dented to shit. Couple more skulls and it'll be worthless. That reminds me." I grab the bat and start to run it under the tap, letting the blood circle around the drain.

We both jump at the sound of the coffee shop's security shutter lifting from the ground, and I cringe at the loud rattle of the metal as it rolls up. That noise will carry all the way down the street.

"Quiet!" hisses Kate as a figure ducks under the half open shutter. It's Arnold, the retired firefighter who holed up with Kate in the antique store. It's no time to bring it up, but if I saw him in the street I'd probably ask for his autograph. He's the spitting image of Danny Glover. It's just uncanny. I swear, if he tells me he's too old for this shit I'll start looking for the hidden cameras.

"Sorry 'bout that," Arnold replies meekly, rolling it back down behind him much more carefully. When it reaches the ground he turns to us and grins. "Got my gun."

Kate smiles, relieved. "And the radio?"

"Police scanner," he corrects, shaking his head. "It's wired up to the car. Couldn't bring it along without lugging the battery with me, but I managed to pick up a little chatter before the signal dropped. It's just like I said, alright. They took down the bridge. Smart motherfuckers."

I look from Kate to Arnold, confused. "What are you talking about?"

Arnold walks to the open chiller cabinet, grabs a Coke and cracks it open with a hiss. "Brooklyn Bridge, son. They took it down, right in the center. That's why it's so quiet hereabouts." He shakes his head in wonder.

"I tell ya, I never thought they'd go through with it."

I feel like I'm missing something, like I'm only hearing one side of a conversation. I turn to Kate with a questioning look.

"Tom wasn't here earlier, Arnold, remember? Why don't you catch him up?" Kate speaks to him like she'd speak to a senile grandpa, and I wonder if Arnold is quite all there. He looks at me blankly for a moment, as if he's forgotten I'm here, then the brightness returns to his eyes.

"Oh, right, right. Sorry, senior moment." He lowers himself to a stool and sets his Coke on the counter. "You remember Bangkok, right?"

I nod. "Of course I remember. Millions of people died."

"Sure, sure. OK, well, after Bangkok the government started planning contingencies in case of an attack. You know, crazy blue sky shit they never thought they'd really need, like what to do if aliens invade and whatnot. That was how they came up with...

Oh, what's it called? That old fairy tale with the guy who lured all those rats and kids away with his... what, like a magic flute or some shit?" He creases his brow for a moment, deep in thought. "Pied piper!"

I shoot a worried glance to Kate, but she shakes her head almost imperceptibly. *Don't worry, he's cool.*

Arnold continues, growing more agitated and jittery with each word. "Operation Pied Piper, they called it. See, they figured these things, you know, they're probably pretty dumb, right? Not too much going on in the old brain box, so they must be easy to trick. They figured they'd probably be attracted to sound, so they came up with this plan to clear the city after an attack." He runs his hand across his stubble. "God damn genius, whoever came up with it."

"What? What was the plan?" I ask, impatiently.

Arnold grins. "Blow the bridges. Wash the fuckers down the river like flushing a gutter. You get it?"

I shake my head. Am I just being dumb, or is this old guy making no sense at all?

Arnold swells his chest proudly. "I was a firefighter. Marine Company One. Twen'y eight years on the *John D. McKean*, and six more on *Three Forty Three*. We were part of all sorts of crazy plans, but Pied Piper jumped out at me more than most. See, in the event of an attack it was the job of *Three Forty Three* to drop anchor right between the Brooklyn and Manhattan bridges after they were blown. *Firefighter II* would go to Williamsburg, and *Bravest* would head up to Queensboro." He notices my blank expression. "Those are the names of our fireboats, son."

"We had these, you know, huge speakers, like you get at a music festival. Big, bulky things. Good and loud, so the sound carries. We were supposed to rig them up and play all sorts of shit to lure those things out to the edge of the bridge and get 'em to jump in. Didn't really matter what, so long as it was loud. Looks like they went with the fireworks track."

It takes me a minute to figure it out. "You mean that noise about an hour ago? That was the boat? I thought it was gunfire."

Arnold shakes his head. "Nope, that was a recording of July 4th. 2011, if I remember right. Personally I would have gone with Springsteen, but I guess it doesn't matter, so long as it worked." He sits back and takes a smug sip of his Coke, as if he came up with the plan himself. "So you see now, right? That was the plan. Blow the bridges, then draw those bastards into the water with the noise, right off the edge into the middle of the East river. Hey presto, you got an empty street outside instead of a million homicidal bastards trying to break in through that shutter."

I frown. "But what about everyone downstream? What happens to them when thousands of those things float ashore?"

Arnold chuckles. "A net, son. A really big goddamn net. Last year, just before I called it a day, we helped set up one of those huge things they use on fishing trawlers. You know the ones, those massive factory ships that drag them back for miles and just hoover up every fucking thing? We got one of those bad boys running right across the Narrows a couple of miles downriver. You just winch that up to the surface and you got yourself a nice little barrier."

I can't help but be impressed. "That's... OK, that's really damned clever. So, do you know what comes next? Is there a second part of the plan, or did they stop at the big net?"

Arnold gives me a toothy grin. "I'll tell you if you hand me one of those cigarettes." He juts his chin towards the pack of Marlboros resting on the counter. I chuckle, slip one from the pack for myself then slide it over to him. "Help yourself."

He lights up, and closes his eyes as he takes a long, blissful pull. "God *damn*, I miss that." He holds the cigarette up and looks lovingly at the smoldering tip. "Marcy - that's my wife, Marcy - she made me quit when I retired. Told me she wanted to keep me around until I'd finished repainting the kitchen. I don't suppose it makes much difference now, right? Chances are none of us will be around long enough for a little smoke to hurt us."

He takes another long drag, coughs and winces. "Looks like I'm out of practice." He sets the cigarette down on the lip of the counter and takes a sip of his Coke. "Prospect Park. That's what's next." He turns his eyes up to the ceiling, trying to summon his memory. "Prospect, Lincoln and James J Braddock. Oh, and the Bronx Zoo. That's where they'll set up rally points for the city. They've all got fresh water, and they'll bring in generators, food, tents and what not. Gotta keep the city empty until the army can sweep it clean, so I guess we'll all be sleeping on camp beds for a while." He shrugs his sleeve up and takes a look at his watch. "That's where Marcy will be waiting, God willing. We live a few blocks from Prospect, and she knows to head there when everything goes to shit." He stubs out his cigarette on the table. "On that note, kids, I think it's high time we mosey."

I turn to Kate. "You good to go?"

She nods and grabs her jacket, but I sense some hesitation.

"What's up?" I ask.

"It's nothing," Kate replies, lowering her voice. "Just... let's talk just the two of us when we get out, OK? There's something you should know."

I nod, and I'm about to reply when Arnold grabs his gun, tucks it into his jacket pocket and lifts himself from his stool with a sharp gasp. "You OK, Arnold?"

"Yeah, yeah," he replies, waving away my concern. "Nothing to worry yourself about."

Kate shoots me a wide eyed look, as if to draw my attention to something. She nods towards Arnold, but I don't get it.

"OK, let's move, kids. Time's wasting."

That's when I see it, as Arnold turns from us towards the shutter. He's bleeding. The back of his right thigh is stained red where he put his weight on the stool. The blood has seeped through his gray trousers, and the sodden material clings to his leg. He doesn't have a limp, but from the look of the blood his injury is more than just a little cut.

Kate takes my arm as Arnold raises the shutter, and she silently mouths the words to me.

He got bit.

****

We drive slowly south on Flatbush, Arnold feathering the gas just enough to keep us rolling without building up the revs. Even driving carefully the engine sounds worryingly loud in the otherwise silent streets.

"Where are all the people?" I ask, peering down the empty roads at each intersection. "How come we're not seeing many bodies? I've only seen a couple in the last five blocks."

Kate shrugs. "Saturday morning. I guess most of them were still in bed when it started. I know the coffee shop was pretty dead. And it was raining pretty bad this morning. Maybe they waited for the crowd to pass then headed for the park?"

"Maybe," I agree. "Maybe a lot of them got out of town before it all went bad. What time did it come on the news?"

Kate shrugs. "I don't know. We don't have a TV in the shop. First I heard of it was a couple of customers talking about a riot going on in Manhattan, then it all went to shit pretty quickly."

Arnold slows the car to maneuver around a mail van blocking our side of the road, and I turn to the townhouses at the sidewalk. "Wait a minute," I mumble. "You seeing this, guys?"

I point out the window to the houses. Almost every second door is wide open, and as we slowly coast by I can see the carnage within. Behind each door a long hallway stretches towards the back of the house, and in almost every one bodies lie, twisted and broken, like chocolates revealed from behind the windows of a macabre advent calendar.

"Jesus, they were all caught at home," mutters Kate, crossing herself as she spots the beaten body of a small boy in SpongeBob pajamas He's lying halfway across the threshold, as if he was trying to escape when he died. He'd look like he was sleeping if it wasn't for the fact that his left leg is broken and twisted forward at the knee, like an ostrich.

I shiver despite the warmth of the car. I can imagine it all too well. Waking up to the sound of a crowd running outside. Rushing down to the front door to check out the commotion, only discovering what was going on when it was too late. When they were already through the door. Already beating, tearing and biting. Who knows how many died in their nightgowns? How many were killed before they even awoke?

Thank fuck I live on a dead end street.

This must be why I didn't see anything on the way to the coffee shop. Our place is in an old, sketchy industrial neighborhood that used to be home to a few small factories and warehouses. It's in the process of being gentrified, but right now the buildings are mostly boarded up and gutted. If the infected are attracted to sound, or light, or... I don't know, the smell of humans there wasn't much to draw them to my little cul-de-sac. They must have flowed right by as I slept, drawn by the sound of the fireworks from the boats on the river.

"Heads up, kids." Arnold tears me back from my imagination. "We got action here." He points ahead, a little further down the arrow straight Flatbush to the intersection with 7th Avenue. A truck trailer has been pulled most of the way across the road, its rear pushed up against the front window of a Duane Reade, leaving a gap just large enough for a car to pass between the truck and the stores on the other side of the street. On top of the trailer a couple of soldiers - or, at least, guys who look like soldiers to my untrained eye - stand and watch us. One peers through a set of binoculars for a long moment then turns and speaks to his partner, who lifts a hand and waves us closer.

Arnold pulls the car forward at a little more than walking pace until we're just a few car lengths from the trailer, and one of the soldiers holds up a hand then waves it in a circle. *Roll down your window.*

"Do you have any injured?" he calls out.

Arnold pokes his head out the window and calls back. "What was that? Speak up, son."

The soldier leans forward and yells. "Any injured? Anyone bitten? No injured allowed."

Arnold turns to Kate with a questioning look. She looks at me for approval, then gives him a nod. "It's OK, we won't tell." Fuck that. I'm sure they're hurting for medical supplies in there, but we're not about to leave Arnold to fend for himself out here for the sake of a little bite.

"Uh uh," he calls back. "Nobody here but us chickens. You got survivors in the park? I'm looking for my wife."

The soldier doesn't answer. He lifts a radio and speaks into it for a moment before turning back to us. "Turn right on 7th," he yells, his voice echoing across the street. "Then continue forward to 9th Street and add your car to the roadblock."

At that he waves us through with his gun. Arnold doesn't wait for anything else. He shifts the car into gear and drives quickly through the gap, his face glistening with sweat and his breathing heavy.

"Thank you," he says in a quiet, shaky voice. "I know you should have turned me in." He shifts in his seat and winces at the pain. The cream leather beneath him squeaks as he moves, and I see it's stained red. "Don't worry, Marcy'll know to have brought a first aid kit. No need to waste supplies patching up an old timer like me."

We slowly drive down 7th Avenue, and for the first time since the moment I flicked on the TV this morning I almost feel safe. At each intersection the street is blocked by cars and trucks, some of them piled on top of one another. They must have some kind of heavy plant nearby to shift the vehicles, I figure, or they've recruited the Hulk to help them build their roadblocks.

This continues all the way down to 9th Street, where a yellow JCB with an enormous scoop slowly levers an old cab up onto its hood until it finally falls, upside down, on top of a beautiful silver Porsche 911 ragtop. I can't help but wince as I watch the windshield cave in under the weight of the cab. It feels like such a waste. The street is thronged with old beaters. Couldn't they have spared the nice cars?

A young soldier flags us down, and Kate rolls down her window.

"OK, guys, you can just pull it into that gap right there." He points to a break in the cars by the Porsche. "Wedge it as best you can, understand?"

Arnold leans over Kate and berates the soldier. "Son, I've been driving this car fifteen years. She's like a *child* to me. Why don't you just use one of these other cars and leave her be?"

The soldier shoulders his rifle and leans in the window. He looks like a twelve year old pre-shaver, but he does his best to stick out his chin and act like a tough guy. "Because, *sir*, we don't have the keys to these cars. It takes ten minutes for this fucking earthmover to push each one onto the pile, and I need to get this street secured by sundown. Now shut up and wedge the damned car."

Arnold turns away from the soldier and puts the car in gear. "Sorry, Bessie," he sighs, pulling it slowly into the gap. "I guess this is where we part ways." He coasts it gently up to the Porsche and stops a couple of feet from the front bumper. "You were a good girl." He pats the wheel and cuts off the engine with a sigh.

The young soldier turns back from his work directing the JCB and calls out. "Pull it in closer, old timer. I want it wedged right up against that Porsche. No gaps."

Arnold reluctantly restarts the engine, shifts into gear and slowly, gently pulls the car a few more inches closer before putting it back into park. There's still a solid six inches of space between the vehicles.

"Jesus!" yells the kid. "We're making a roadblock here. Stop being so fucking precious about it. Pull. It. *Closer.*"

Arnold shuts off the engine and calls out. "You know what, fuck you, kid. This is my damned car."

"Easy now, Arnold," I warn, resting my hand on his shoulder. "We don't want any trouble, OK? We have bigger things to worry about than a car."

My words have no effect. Arnold seems to have slipped into that recalcitrant state shared by crotchety old people and little kids who flat out refuse to eat their vegetables. I'm sure he knows deep down that he's acting irrationally. He knows it's crazy to try to protect a car when the world is collapsing around him, but he's been pushed too far by an uppity kid holding a gun, and now he won't move another inch. He crosses his arms and stares down the soldier.

"Oh, for the love of God," the kid sighs. He pulls his rifle down from his shoulder and holds it menacingly, pointed at the asphalt in front of the car. "I'll do it myself. Get out of the car, sir." Arnold stares straight ahead and tightens his arms. "Get out of the car *now*."

With the final word he lifts the muzzle of the gun and points it directly through the window at Arnold. Kate flinches in the front passenger seat and lets out a panicked cry. She grabs Arnold by the arm and shakes him. "Do what he says, for God's sake! Arnold, this is crazy!"

Kate's voice seems to get through to the old guy more effectively than the gun pointed at his head. He looks at her and sighs, slowly uncrossing his arms, and mumbles. "It's just..." I can't see his eyes from the back seat, but I can hear tears in his quivering voice. "Bessie belonged to my son." He places both hands on the wheel and holds it tight, like he's holding the hands that used to rest there. "He didn't leave much when he went to Iraq, but I promised him I'd take care of her until..." his breath catches in his throat, "until he came home to us. And I always did. Washed her every Sunday, rain or shine. Kept her running smooth." He looks up at Kate with tears in his eyes. "It's what James would have wanted, you know?"

Shit.

The young soldier moves closer, the stock of his gun pressed up against his shoulder. He taps the barrel against the window. "Get out *now*," he orders. I can see the barrel shaking a little. This kid has probably never fired a shot in anger. There's fear in his voice. Panic. His finger twitches over the trigger. He's liable to do something stupid.

I slowly, carefully push open the back door, making sure not to startle the kid, but he still wheels around on me, the gun pointed right at my face. "*Woah, woah, unarmed!* Steady now, there's no problem. I'm stepping out of the car, OK? Please don't fire." I hold my hands palms forward above the door and slowly climb out, taking care not to make any sudden movements. When I'm finally on my feet I gently push the door closed and take two long steps back towards the trunk of the car, just to make sure the kid doesn't think I'll make a lunge for him.

"Please, sir, can you just give him a minute to say goodbye?" I plead. I realize how stupid this sounds, but I guess there's no other option. "Look, this was his son's car, and the kid died in the Gulf. He's not trying to be an asshole, it's just his last connection with his kid. You're a soldier, you must understand what it's like for the parents. Can you give him a break? Please?"

The kid's eyes dart from me to Arnold and back again. His finger is still on the trigger and the barrel is still shaking like crazy. I'm terrified that the the slightest breeze might make him twitch. I've never had a gun pointed in my face before. My adrenaline is spiking, and I can feel my heart thump in my chest. It takes all my strength to avoid ducking behind the car, but I know the slightest move might set him off.

Time passes. Who knows how long? Every second feels like an hour with that barrel pointing at my nose, but eventually I see the kid's trigger finger relax a little. The hyper, agitated look fades from his eyes, and he slowly lowers the gun. I can *feel* it running down my body as the barrel moves, tracing a line from my head to my feet. I don't dare take a breath until it's finally pointed at the ground.

"OK," the kid sighs, nodding. "I'll give him one minute."

I duck my head down and look into the car. Kate's comforting Arnold. His shoulders are shaking, and his head is pressed against the steering wheel.

"Thank you," I sigh, taking a long, shuddering breath. "I really appreciate it. I'm Tom." I hold out my hand, but pull it back when I see the kid take a tighter grip on his gun. "Umm... Can I offer you a cigarette?" I point to my pocket, and with slow, exaggerated movements reach in and pull out the pack.

"Karl," the soldier replies, still a little nervous. "I don't smoke."

"OK, well I do, and if I don't have one now I might have a coronary. You sure know how to make a guy shit himself." I let out a little chuckle, and start to relax when I see a shy, embarrassed smile appear on the kid's face.

"Sorry about that," he says, speaking like a human for the first time. "Rough day, you know? Between you and me I'm scared out of my mind."

I nod in agreement. "You and me both. I'm still hoping I'll wake up soon. This has to be some kind of fucking nightmare, right?" I light my cigarette and point to his fatigues. "So what are you? Army? Navy?" There are a couple of patches on his shoulders, but nothing I recognize as a branch or rank.

Karl looks down at his uniform, seemingly embarrassed. "Umm..." he mumbles, "JROTC."

I shake my head. "Sorry, I'm pretty clueless about the military. What's that?"

His cheeks burn red. "Junior Reserve Officers' Training Corps," he mumbles quietly, suddenly looking like even more of a scared kid. All of his bluster has evaporated. "I'm in high school. I'm just a cadet." He shakes his rifle. "I've never even used one of these. We train with old M1 Garands, and I never even used live ammo before..." His voice trails off. His lower lip starts to quiver for a moment, but he manages to pull himself together. "And now they've put me in charge of building this roadblock. Just me and Gary." He points to the guy in the cab of the JCB, carefully maneuvering his scoop beneath another car. "I just wanna go home. I don't wanna do this any more."

I don't really know what to say to that. "There's nobody else who could help?"

The kid laughs bitterly and shakes his head. "Last I heard there was a unit from Fort Dix coming to relieve us, but that was three hours ago. Who the fuck knows what happened to them between there and here?"

"So who's in charge?"

Karl snorts. "Some Lieutenant Colonel. I
don't know his name. *In charge* might be the
wrong phrase, though. There are only a
couple of dozen soldiers. *Real* soldiers, I
mean, from the 69th. Most of the battalion
was deployed months ago. There's only a
couple hundred reservists left behind, and
they're spread pretty thin across the city.
Most of the guys here are either retired
veterans or cadets, like me." He looks down
at his oversized fatigues. "We got plenty of
uniforms, but no soldiers to fill them."

"Jesus," I gasp, suddenly acutely aware of
just how exposed we are here in the street. "I
thought this was some kind of huge military
operation. You know, battleships off the
coast, jets flying overhead, that sort of thing.
You're telling me it's just a few guys and an
earthmover?"

Karl leans back against the hood of a
wrecked car and rests his rifle against the
tire. "Yeah, pretty much. I'm only here
because I live down the street in
Bensonhurst. Guy on the news said FEMA
was setting up a camp in the park, but when

me and my dad got here there was only the colonel and a few guys. No sign of FEMA anywhere. It's FUBAR. We're blocking up the streets as best we can, but who knows what comes next? We don't have any tents. No cots. No medical supplies. The only food we got is whatever we can find in the stores behind the roadblocks, and who knows how long that'll last?"

I get the feeling Karl is only holding onto his cool by a slender thread, and I can't blame him. I can't imagine what it must feel like for someone his age to be handed a gun and told to defend a bunch of helpless civilians. He looks like he could burst into tears at any moment. I don't want to push him, but I need to understand the situation. "How many people came to the park?"

The kid shrugs. "Too many to count. Hundreds of them. Maybe a few thousand. The man said on the news... you know, we just thought it'd all be OK if we came down. He said it'd be safe for us here." He turns away from me, embarrassed, and wipes a tear from his cheek. "And now all I can think is how safe can we be if kids like me are in charge of building the roadblocks, you know? The situation's gotta be pretty desperate, right?"

I drop my cigarette and crush it beneath my boot. "Well, you look to be doing a damned good job to me, Karl. I'm sure you'll make a fine officer. Your dad will be proud." I feel dumb saying those words. I don't have a clue if he's doing a good job, but he seems to straighten his back a little at the compliment. He rubs his moist eyes and smiles awkwardly.

"Thanks," he mumbles, embarrassed. He stands and points to the car. "OK, we better get this thing moved. You think he's had enough time?"

I nod. "Yeah, that should be enough. Thanks, Karl."

I walk to the driver's door of the car and tap on the window. Arnold's head is still resting against the steering wheel, but he seems to have stopped crying.

No response. I tap again, but still he doesn't move. I pull open the door.

"Come on, Arnold. It's time." I place my hand on his shoulder, but I can tell right away that something isn't quite right. Something... I can't put my finger on it, but the hairs suddenly stand up on the back of my neck. There's something I'm missing. Something my conscious mind hasn't noticed.

"Arnold? Hey, buddy, can you..." My voice trails off as it finally clicks. I can feel Arnold's muscles moving beneath my hand. They're... rippling. Tensing. Bunching together as if he's preparing himself to get up. But he's not breathing. His chest isn't moving. Hasn't moved since I opened the door.

"Kate," I whisper quietly, barely loud enough to drown out the sudden thumping of my heart. "Get out of the car, honey. Quickly."

Kate looks up at me with a a puzzled expression. "What—"

"*Now*, Kate," I hiss. "Get out *now*."

She doesn't see what's going on, but the urgency in my voice makes her move quickly. She turns and fumbles for the door handle, but beneath my hand I can feel Arnold's muscles twitch and quiver like there's a light current passing through his body. I tighten my grip, pressing his shoulder down as best I can.

"Kate, *get out!*" I yell.

She finally pushes open the door and tumbles out into the street as Arnold lifts his head from the steering wheel, moving as if I wasn't even holding him down. Kate kicks her door closed and the old man's head snaps around to chase the sound, giving me the chance to back away and slam the driver's door.

Now he turns back to me, and my fears are confirmed. This isn't Arnold any more. The twinkle has gone from his eyes. They're just blank now; dark, unfocused orbs surrounded by ashy skin, hunting for the next target.

I back away from the car slowly, remembering the little girl I saw in the Prius. I figure I can keep him from attacking if I just move slowly enough, but he proves me wrong. The moment I move a muscle he launches himself at the window, his muffled bellow drowned out by the sound of the JCB engine droning by the roadblock.

"Karl!" I yell, stumbling back away from the car. "Shoot him!"

The kid grabs up his rifle, but doesn't point it at the car. "I can't!" he cries.

I turn to him, grab his shoulders and roughly shake him. "Karl, fucking shoot him!"

The terrified kid lifts his gun up to me and flips it over. "*I can't!*" he yells again. "It's loaded with fucking blanks!" He points to the magazine. "It's a training rifle. We don't have enough ammo to go around!"

"Oh *Jesus*. Some fucking safe zone." Arnold continues to throw himself against the door, and I just know it won't hold out long. A crack has already appeared in the window and it's spreading with every blow.

I look around for my bat, and swear under my breath as I realize I left it on the back seat of the car. Far too risky to try to get it back now. The kid's rifle might make a half decent club, but something tells me Arnold will take more killing than the guy back in the antique store. He's an old man but he has a good few inches on me, a barrel chest and thick arms. I can only imagine what would happen if he got the chance to launch himself at me.

I cast my eyes around the street and panic for a moment when I realize Kate has vanished from beside the car. It's not until I hear her yell that I realize what's going on.

"Get out of the way!" I look up and see Kate clinging onto the cab door of the earthmover, waving me aside. The driver turns the wheel and powers forward towards the car, and as the enormous tires bump against it he pushes a lever and sends the heavy scoop pressing down.

I run towards the earthmover and yell out for the driver to stop, but the sound of the hydraulics drowns out my voice. I can see right away that his plan to crush Arnold won't work. The scoop isn't nearly large enough. It only reaches halfway across the car, and as it pushes down, bending the steel frame with a tortured squeal, the weakened driver's side window bursts outwards.

Arnold squirms his way out through the window, falling to the ground as the bench seat of the car folds and cracks. His foot is caught for a moment in the twisted door frame and I imagine I can hear the ankle snap as the crushed frame pins it, but he pulls his foot clear with a yank, tearing off a shoe and leaving a bloody smear down the side of the door.

I watch, helpless, as he pulls himself to his feet and breaks into a limping run, closing the dozen feet between him and the frozen, petrified kid in the space of a single breath. Karl holds up his gun like a shield, but it does nothing to stop Arnold. The old man takes the kid down like a bowling pin. They both vanish behind a car, and as the engine of the earthmover cuts out I hear Karl's frantic, petrified screams, broken by dull thumps that sound like a meat tenderizer slapping against a steak. The screams gurgle and fade until the thumps are all that's left. Steady. Regular. The sound of Arnold's fists pounding against Karl's lifeless body.

"We have to get out of here, *now*," I whisper, holding my hand up to Kate. She takes it and climbs quickly down from the JCB. "You too," I say, nodding at the guy in the cab. "Get out of there."

The guy clings to the steering wheel and shakes his head frantically. He's too scared to speak.

"Get down *now*," I hiss, pointing at the ground. *What the fuck is with this guy?*

The driver leans over and grabs the edge of the door. "Fuck that," he says, shaking his head frantically. Before I can stop him he pulls the door closed, shutting himself, in, and the clapping sound of steel on steel rings out across the street. The thing that used to be Arnold stands from behind the car and swings his head towards us.

I don't wait to see what happens next. I hop down from the cab, grab Kate by the hand and set off east at a dead run, the JCB blocking us from Arnold's sight. Behind me I hear him wail, and as we sprint I have just enough sense to feel ashamed that my first thought is to hope he'll pick the driver as a target before us.

We've cleared around ten car lengths by the time I hear the JCB engine sputter back to life. I risk a quick look behind me, and I'm horrified enough by the sight to come to a halt. The vehicle plows forward towards the roadblock as Arnold climbs clumsily up the side. I don't hear the driver's scream above the sound of the engine, but I can imagine it clearly enough as Arnold forces his way through the open window and into the cab. His legs vanish inside as the JCB hits the roadblock, pushing the cars aside with ease, opening up the road to anyone - any*thing* - that might try to come through.

Kate grabs my hand and pulls. "Come *on!*" she cries. "There's nothing we can do for him."

I start sprinting again, struggling to keep pace with Kate as she tears away towards the park. My throat burns with each breath. My legs ache but I keep going, following Kate until we reach Prospect Park West, pass through the gate and burst through into the park. We sprint by a parking lot to our left, through a row of bushes and out onto a broad tree lined jogging trail. Still we run, following the path through the silent, empty park. We pass the baseball diamonds where I play with a team from my local bar every Sunday. We turn left at the calm, peaceful lily pond where I walked with Kate after our first date, then through a copse of thick, dense trees until we burst out onto the broad field where families picnic every warm day through the summer.

We slow. I almost stumble and trip over my feet as I break out of the sprint into a jog, then a walk. Finally I stop, gaping in awe at the sight ahead of us.

The field is full. Bursting with people, with barely a blade of grass to be seen among the thronged crowd. Old people. Little kids. Husbands. Wives. Families. Thousands of them stretching as far as the eye can see, just sitting there as if this is a regular Saturday afternoon. As if they're here for a picnic, and they're about to fire up the barbecue and toss a football.

And barely a soldier in sight. Just a few guys in fatigues overwhelmed by countless civilians. Not a single APC. No Humvees. No tanks. Not even an old Willy's Jeep.

These people are sitting ducks.

They're all going to die.

****

Food?

Arnold rolls himself from the body of the driver and lands awkwardly in the gap between the seat and the door. His body doesn't seem to be responding to his commands quite as well as it did just a little while ago. Everything feels a little... creaky, like old, rusted hinges. There's no pain, though. His body just feels numb.

His head is foggy, too, like everything has gone a little soft and fuzzy around the edges. Everything apart from the hunger, that is. And the rage. Both are painfully sharp, like needles digging into his brain.

He rests his back against the door and watches the body for a moment, like a cat watches a dead mouse, waiting - hoping - for it to start moving again. His fists open and close, ready to launch into it once again at the first twitch.

His heart isn't really in it now, though. The body had seemed so attractive just a few moments ago, with its yelling and squirming, back when it had been... different. It had been irresistible. The noises it made sent Arnold's brain fizzing. The way it tried to scramble out one window as Arnold climbed in the other both excited and enraged him. The sound and movement were like catnip. He just couldn't resist reaching out and grabbing it, catching it by the belt of its pants and pulling it back into the cab. He couldn't resist pounding until it stopped struggling. It was... satisfying.

Now, though? Not so much. It just lays there like a rag doll. Still. Grey. Dull. Arnold reaches out and touches it, hoping against hope the movement will start again. If it starts again maybe he can take a bite this time. It seemed so enticing just a moment ago, but now the body holds little interest.

Still it refuses to move.

And still.

Still nothing. This is getting boring now.

Moldy bread.

The random synaptic misfires that pass for thought in what's left of Arnold's mind dredge up a dusty old memory, back from... back from before, the other time. The memory plays out in his head like a foreign movie without the subtitles. He doesn't really understand the nuance, but he can just about grasp the general drift.

He's standing in a dark room, carefully, quietly reaching for things. Bags. Jars. Knives. He's putting something together in the darkness by feel, remembering where everything is kept. He moves slowly, trying not to make too much noise. Two slices of bread with something between them. Tasty. He's been looking forward to this for hours.

He lifts the thing to his mouth and takes a big bite. Chews. Chews again, then stops. Something tastes wrong. He reaches out to the wall and pushes something, and suddenly the room is painfully bright. He squints his eyes for a moment until they adjust to the light. He looks down at the thing in his hands, and suddenly he understands the problem. The bread is covered in gray and green patches of mold

Mold is wrong. Doesn't belong there. Shouldn't eat.

It's in his mouth, wet and mashed up and sticky and disgusting, pressed into the gaps between his teeth. Stuck in the crevice where a molar cracked and rotted to the root years ago. Deep in there, where his probing tongue can never reach. Where only a toothpick can free it. He gags, bends over the counter and spits the wet, mashed glob onto the white surface, but he can still taste it. He can still feel the texture of the mold, sticking to him like a sheet of rice paper pressed against the roof of his mouth.

He gags again, but this time he feels the vomit rise up his throat, hot and stinging. It splashes on the counter and the liquid brings with it thick, wet chunks that stick in his throat on the way up. Something goes the wrong way and lodges somewhere deep in his sinuses. He can smell it. He tastes it in his throat. He can *feel* it there, coating his tongue. He presses a finger against a nostril and snorts, trying to dislodge the chunk stuck deep in his nose, but it only makes him retch even harder.

He tries to make it to the basin before the next wave arrives, but he doesn't move quickly enough. Another retch, and the fresh puke joins the rest with a sickening splash on the countertop. Above his gasps he hears the dull, wet spatter of liquid dripping from the counter to the linoleum below. Thick, acrid bile burns his throat as his vision swims through tearful eyes, and a bubble of spit and puke bursts on his lips as he gasps.

The movie stops playing, and now Arnold understands. The thing next to him is like moldy bread. He thought it was good, but it's not good. Not now. Now it's gross. Gone bad. Don't eat. Only eat the fresh ones. Only eat the ones that move.

He lashes out and pushes the body further away, suddenly disgusted with it. It slumps against the door of the cab and the head dangles out the open window on its broken neck, like a baseball glued to a Slinky.

It's still too close for comfort. Arnold doesn't want to be trapped in here with it a moment longer. He's... *scared* isn't quite the right word, but it's close enough to describe the confused stew of instinct, impulse and childlike emotion running through a brain that's operating on little more than the stem. He twists his body to the right and sees the door he entered through. There's some sort of catch on it, a black steel stick jutting out from the shiny yellow door. Some dim half-memory tells him he could use it to make the door swing open, but he seems to have forgotten exactly how that would work. No matter. The window is open. He can still think clearly enough to know he can squirm through the gap to escape just as he squirmed through it to enter.

It seems a little more difficult this time. He moves more slowly now he isn't so excited, and his clothes keep catching on things. It takes a long while, but eventually he gets enough of his weight over the edge of the window to tumble out and fall back to the street. He lands on his shoulder and hears something snap, but still there's no pain. He's just numb.

Arnold stands slowly, using the side of the earthmover for support. He can't really turn his head to the right now. When he tries he feels like there's something blocking him. There's something wrong with his right foot, too. He looks down and sees pink and white bone just above his ankle, jutting out from the side like a sharp blade. The foot is bent inwards, and his weight rests on its side. He can still walk, though. After just a few clumsy steps the bone has torn through enough skin that he can rest his weight on the pointed tip. It crumbles a little, but soon enough it seems to smooth to a decent stump. The foot drags uselessly behind it like a sad, deflated balloon.

Up ahead he sees another body slumped against a car. Small. Dressed in oversized fatigues, the chest and face caved in, and the light brown desert camo scheme of his jacket darkened with blood. Arnold curls his lip in disgust and makes sure to stay well away from it. Moldy bread. Bad. What a waste. He's hungry now. Famished.

He bumps up against something hard and turns quickly, ready to fight. It's a car, the roof crushed down almost flat. Another memory tries to break through, but this one doesn't come with a movie. It's just a vague hint of a thought, like a dream that seemed so vivid just a moment ago but now slips just out of reach. Something about this car was important, but it doesn't look like there's anything of interest there now. Just a little smear of blood down the side of the door. It doesn't look appetizing.

There were more here. More... what's the word? People. They were in the car. He dips his head beneath the bent door frame and peers into the wreckage curiously, but the broken seats are empty. They were here. He knows they were here, but now they're not here. His mind no longer has a firm grasp on the concept of time, but the randomly firing mass of flesh still works well enough to tell him that the people must have gone somewhere since he last saw them.

But where?

His head jerks up at a distant sound carried on the breeze. Some kind of high pitched feedback squeal, somewhere far away. He turns his head this way and that, trying to home in on the noise. It seems to be coming from everywhere, bouncing through the streets and echoing off the walls. There's no way to tell—

No, wait. There it is. It's coming from somewhere ahead. Through the broken line of cars and down the long, straight road. Whatever it is it's coming from that direction. That's where he has to go. He can feel that fizzing sensation return.

His head spins around at another sound behind him, but he quickly sees that it's nothing to get excited about. It's just another one of them. Hungry. Angry. Excited. Can't eat it, though. The smell isn't right. Another one appears from behind a car, and then another off in the distance from around a corner, far behind. They all heard the sound, and they're all moving in the same direction. Some can move faster than him. Some aren't so broken. Some don't have to drag a useless foot behind them. It makes him angry to see them walking faster. Jealous. The other ones might get there before him, and all the food will be gone.

He sets off as quickly as he can move, dragging himself towards the distant sound. It's stopped now but he remembers the direction it came from. All he can hear now is the slow, steady click and grind of his bone against the asphalt, and the low, curious groans of the others quickly catching up to him.

He's excited now, but he doesn't know how to show it. His mouth doesn't seem to work like it used to. He wants to speak, but all he can do is groan.

No matter. He'll get to eat soon.

****

I can't help but think of 9/11.

I remember I'd turned eleven years old a few days earlier, and my party had marked the end of a long, glorious, lazy summer. The school year had officially begun the previous day, September 10th, but my first day back been postponed for a week thanks to some emergency with the plumbing in the cafeteria. I didn't really give a damn about the reason, I was just over the moon to get a bonus vacation week. It felt like magical extra time had been conjured up out of thin air, just like when as an adult you wake up thinking it's time for work, then feel that soft, warm little thrill when you look at the clock and realize you still have two more hours to sleep. It was fucking fantastic. One more precious week of waking up late and watching cartoons in my pajamas

Unfortunately my mother had other plans. She had to go to work, and since couldn't find a sitter on short notice I was packed off to my great uncle's deli on Fulton Street, a weird little place that stank to high heaven of pickled beets and, forever creeping from the little cubby behind the stock room, stale cigar smoke. Mom said a week of honest work would be character building, much more valuable than anything I'd learn at school, and she was right. By the start of my second day I'd already learned an important life lesson: the smell of pickled beets and old cigar smoke makes me gag.

I was sneaking in a quick nap on the toilet when Flight 11 hit the north tower, really stretching out that first crap of the day as long as I could, hoping my uncle wouldn't knock on the door and make me help out in the store. I'd been in there for twenty minutes when I heard a dull rumble and felt the room shake a little. I remember the mirror trembled on the wall, and my reflection blurred for a moment. I had no clue what was going on, of course. No one did, not when it started.

At first I thought a transformer might have blown somewhere nearby. That was usually the answer to any mysterious explosive sound, much to my disappointment. Whenever I heard something potentially exciting I'd always rush as quickly as I could out to the street, hoping I might be lucky enough to find myself faced with a gory car crash or a cool fire, but it was always another damned transformer, overtaxed by the summer heat.

This time was different, of course. By the time I got down to the street there was a confused crowd gathered around. The traffic had stopped in the street, and people were out of their cars and looking up at the sky to the west where a thick, dark shroud had already started to draw over the city like the ash cloud from an erupting volcano. This *never* happened, not in New York. Even if one of those city-sized spacecraft from Independence Day really did hover over the city people would barely break their stride. New Yorkers don't stop unless they're on fire, and even then it'd have to be a big one.

I started to run without thinking. I didn't know what the hell was going on, but I knew this was exciting. Finally something interesting was going down, and I was there to see it. By the time I reached the Hilton on the corner of Fulton and Church I knew this was big, and when the north tower finally hove into view my sprint slowed to a jog, then a walk. Then I just stood there and gawped, like everyone else.

You'd have to have been there to really get how it felt. It was just... confusing. The streets were packed with hundreds of people who'd been attracted by the noise. Thousands. Some stood there and watched. Others tried to get as close as possible. A few ran as fast as their legs could carry them in the opposite direction. People kinda laughed and shook our heads at those guys, because... well, if you run away you're not a real New Yorker, you know? Nobody wants to be thought a tourist. Certainly not me, Brooklyn born and bred, always eager to make it clear that I was a true city boy.

At first it was all a little lighthearted, believe it or not. A couple of people were making dark jokes about... I don't know, something about the Merrill Lynch annual company barbecue. I don't want to make these people sound awful, but you have to understand they didn't have a clue what was going on. Of course they wouldn't have cracked wise if they'd understood what was happening. And again, these were New Yorkers. You don't last long in the city without developing a strong grasp of gallows humor

The jokes stopped when the south tower was hit.

I couldn't see much from where I was standing. The Hilton blocked my view of the south tower, but everyone on the street heard the impact even if they couldn't see it. We suddenly knew that this wasn't a regular fire. This wasn't just some *how was your day, honey?* story people would be telling over the dinner table. This was serious.

Whispers started to pass back through the crowd. Some people nearby said they'd seen a plane through a gap in the buildings, and a couple of minutes later a cab driver said the radio was reporting that a light aircraft had hit the north tower. Those around him corrected him at first, telling him he must be confused. The guys on the ground were saying they'd *just now* seen a plane, right before the south tower erupted in smoke and flame, but the radio seemed to be talking about the first explosion. There can't have been two planes, right?

That's the way it went for the next hour or so. It was just a huge game of Telephone, rumors passing through the crowd as we all watched the towers burn. After a half hour of confusion and fear news of the Pentagon attack rippled down the street. That one came straight from the radio and the TVs playing in the cafes and delis along Fulton, so we assumed it was legit, but other rumors couldn't be so quickly confirmed. There were whispers of an explosion outside the White House, and another at Sears Tower. Someone mentioned something about an attack in London, or maybe Paris. A woman beside me managed to get through to her sister on the phone, and she said there were more planes in the air headed for the city. It was just endless. Rumor upon rumor, rippling through the crowd and carrying waves of fear and confusion along with them.

That's just how I'm feeling now, almost two decades later, standing in the middle of a crowd of thousands in Prospect Park, clutching Kate's hand for dear life. Nobody has any solid information, but in a situation like this rumors flood in to fill the vacuum.

"I've got no bars, is anyone getting any bars?" a guy in a torn suit in front of me calls out. A few around him shake their heads, frowning with concern at their useless phones as if the lack of signal is a greater tragedy than the hordes of murderous creatures roaming the city.

"My sister said the army's taken back Manhattan up to Central Park," a woman claims, waving her phone in the air as if it amounted to proof. "I just got through to her before the signal died."

"Bullshit," grumbles a wiry old man, pointing his cane at the woman. "My son was on the payphone, and he says the news said there's nobody left alive in the city."

The guy in the torn suit takes a knee in front of the old man. "When was this, sir?"

"Just now!" he proclaims. "Ask him yourself, he's right there. Hey, Ron! *Ron*! Come over here and tell 'em what you told me."

The old man's overweight son looks up from a conversation with a young woman and turns in our direction, then slowly makes his way over to us, red faced, overexerted by the short walk.

"Umm," he says, catching his breath. "Yeah, so Fox says they lost contact with D.C. about a half hour ago. They don't know where the President is."

"No, you idiot," the guy's dad scolds, "tell them what's goin' on here."

"Oh right, right," he replies, ignoring the insult. "New York is *gone*." He waves a hand in a slicing motion. "Just... gone, all the way up to, like, Yankee Stadium or something. They sent a traffic chopper over the city and it's just overrun. Corpse city." He lets out a nervous laugh and a woman beside him gasps, reaches out and claps her hands over her kid's ears.

"Jesus," she sobs tearfully. "My husband's in Manhattan. Can you show some damned respect?"

"Umm, sorry ma'am," the guy replies, cowed.

The first woman waves her phone again. "That's not true. My sister just said the army's at Central Park, pushing north."

"What, your sister told you?" the fat guy snorts. "Who are you gonna believe, your sister or Fox News?"

"*Duh*. My sister. Those assholes at Fox are probably just trying to get a bump in the ratings. They'd *love* it if New York was ruined. I bet—" Her voice is drowned out by a painfully loud high pitched squeal as someone switches on the PA system. The sound continues for a solid five seconds before someone pulls the plug and the agonizing feedback cuts out.

I pull Kate away from the group by the hand and lower my voice as we pass through the muttering, gossiping crowd. "OK, we need to get the fuck out of here right now. Let's go."

She tugs back on my hand, drawing to a halt. "What? Why? We're safe here, right? Why the hell would we go back out there?"

I shake my head and lean in closer. "Look... OK, you can't react to what I'm about to say,

OK? I don't want to panic people." I drop my voice to a whisper. "That kid back there, the soldier? His gun was loaded with blanks. He said they don't have enough ammo to go around. These people can't protect us."

Kate shakes her head in disbelief. "What are you talking about? Who told you this?"

"He did. Karl, the kid. He said there's supposed to be an army unit coming up from Fort Dix to secure the safe zone, but they never showed. All they've got is a few reservists and a couple of cadets. This isn't a safe zone. It's all just..." I wave my hand around, searching for the right word. "Theater. It's a fucking *buffet*. Just a few old guys and kids playing soldiers, trying to keep people calm. They can't keep us safe." I look across the field at the thronged crowd. "And look at these people. Look how unprepared they are."

Kate looks around and shrugs her shoulders. "What do you mean?"

"I mean look at these guys." I point to a young family sitting in the shade of a tree nearby. They have a suitcase open before them, their hastily grabbed belongings piled inside. "Look at their stuff. There must be a dozen pairs of heels in that bag. And what's that, an Xbox? Seriously? No food. No water. No weapons. No warm clothes. Just... stuff. Random crap they don't want to get looted. They think they're going straight home once this all blows over, but they're *not*. Those things are coming, *soon*, and even if they don't find us this bunch of morons will tear itself to pieces when they realize there's nothing to *eat*. If FEMA doesn't arrive with water purifiers there'll be nothing to drink, either. They're not prepared for this. Hell, neither are we, but at least we understand how deep in the shit we are."

I nod my head towards a skinny, tearful hipster kid sitting cross legged on his own, clutching a cotton Whole Foods grocery bag to his chest. Peeking from the top I can see dozens of vinyl sleeves.

"Jesus, look at this asshole. Does he thinks he's gonna fight off a bunch of infected with his limited edition Smiths album? Where are all the fucking guns?"

Kate stays silent. We've often argued about the need for stricter gun control - her for, me against. I agreed with her that it was pretty pointless to keep one for home protection, but even though I'm one of those knock-kneed lefty wimps the NRA people laugh at I always insisted they were necessary for just this kind of situation, when the shit hits the fan and law enforcement collapses.

Kate thought that was a crazy idea. Her late father had been a cop, and she couldn't wrap her head around the concept of a world in which he and his kind wouldn't be there to protect us, or might even work against us. A cop had tucked her in every night as a kid, and the idea that the uniform meant anything other than absolute safety just didn't fit with her world view. I could never figure out a way to convince her that the society we knew might not last forever.

It didn't help matters that her dad had been shot and killed in the line of duty when she was twelve. A bodega robbery gone bad. Wrong place at the wrong time. Her opinion on guns was fixed for life on that day.

Just a few months ago, a couple of weeks after she moved into my apartment, I told her we should buy a handgun just in case. Just as last ditch insurance, to be kept locked securely in a glass case marked *break only in the event of the apocalypse.* I told her we could keep the ammo right on the other side of the house. Hell, we could keep the gun in pieces, scattered around the apartment like a damned jigsaw puzzle so it was impossible it could ever be used by accident. She gave me an ultimatum: I could live with her or I could live with a gun, but not both.

I chose her, like an idiot.

I get the feeling now wouldn't be a great time to say I told her so.

"OK, so where do you wanna go?" Kate finally asks. "I'll follow your lead, but I don't want to go back out there without a plan, OK?"

"Agreed," I reply, resisting the urge to rub her nose in it. The last thing I want is to have to face the apocalypse with a girlfriend in a bad mood. "We need information. *Real* information, not this rumor mill crap. Karl told me there was some colonel running the show."

"Babe?"

"If we can find out where he is maybe we can pin him down and get some intel."

"Babe."

"OK, so keep your eye out for one of the soldiers. They must know where to look."

"*Tom!*"

I finally realize she's tugging on my sleeve. "What is it?"

"Follow my finger, genius," she replies, exasperated. "Doesn't that look like somewhere a colonel might hang out?"

I look over in the direction she's pointing, out at the edge of the field. It's the park administration office, a squat gray concrete building with a cell tower climbing from its roof. The front door is wide open, and beside it a soldier stands guard, his M16 hanging from around his neck.

"OK, that looks like a good place to check out," I grudgingly concede, and start walking towards the building. I know it's dumb but my injured pride forces me to open my mouth again. "You were still wrong about gun control, though."

Kate slaps me lightly on the back of my head. "Whatever, babe. Keep walkin'."

****

"Woah woah woah, hold it, guys. The building is off limits." The soldier sidesteps to block the door as we approach, and reaches behind him to pull it closed.

I take a couple of steps back. I'm in no mood to have an M16 pointed at me again today, even if there's a good chance it might be loaded with blanks. "Is the lieutenant colonel inside? We just need to get some information."

"That's affirmative," replies the soldier, hiking his gun up against his chest and staring straight ahead. "And he's far too busy to deal with civilians. What do you need, kid?"

I bristle a little at the word 'kid.' This guy may not be a young cadet like Karl, but he's not all that much older than I am. Maybe mid-thirties, well built with a close cropped head of salt and pepper hair. I check the insignia on his chest and dig through my memory for his rank. "We need to know which direction is safe to get the fuck out of here, Sergeant. We want to get out of the city."

The sergeant shakes his head. "Negative. Orders are to keep civilians within the safe zone perimeter until reinforcements arrive. We need to sweep the whole area before we release anyone. Can't have folks running around the streets while we work. Just relax, OK? You're perfectly safe."

I feel my hands ball into fists at the thought of being detained. "*Safe*? You know this area isn't secure, right? We just came from the roadblock at 9th Street, and I can tell you it's been compromised. At least one of those things is on this side of the barrier. It killed one of your guys. Karl. You know him, Sergeant? He was sent out there with fucking blanks in his gun."

The sergeant's stern expression softens a little, and his shoulders slump from attention. "Karl? Jesus. He was a good kid." He tugs his radio up to his mouth. "Kilo Six, this is Alpha Niner. I have critical intel, copy? Over."

A tinny voice comes back a few seconds later. "Alpha Niner, copy. Send it."

"We have a potential breach at—" He turns to me. "You said 9th Street?" Back to the radio. "9th Street roadblock. Possible man down, possible hostiles within perimeter. Over."

"Roger that, Alpha. I'm aware of the situation. I have two friendlies down, and multiple hostiles have been taken out. Roadblock was breached, but has now been secured. Over."

"Kilo, acknowledged. Alpha out." The sergeant lowers the radio. "See? Nothing to worry about, guys. We got this. Now, I'm going to have to ask you to—"

"*Negative*, Command! We have multiple civilians on site. Confirm your last!" An angry male voice booms through the wooden door, and the sergeant falls silent and turns his head to listen.

"Request recall on those bombers, Command. I got more'n three thousand healthy, uninfected civilians here waiting for an evac route. You have to give them at least *some* chance."

"What's going on?" I ask.

The sergeant holds up his hand to silence me. "Shhh. Hang on." He turns and pushes open the door a couple of inches with his foot, careful not to make any sound, and tilts his head to hear more clearly.

"Sergeant, what's going *on*?" I insist.

He waves me away and hisses impatiently. "Will you shut the fuck up for a minute?"

When I hear the voice through the door again it's much quieter. The anger seems to have vanished, replaced with a dejected acceptance. "Understood, Command," the man sighs. I hear the faint, tinny response, too quiet to make out the words. "No, I'll *do my duty*." Those last words are spat out, a hint of the anger returning. "May God have mercy on you all. Out."

"Fuck." The sergeant pulls his foot back and lets the door swing closed, and when he turns back to us his face has lost all color He grabs his radio and raises it to his mouth, but seems to reconsider before he holds down the button.

"What is it?" Kate demands. "What's going on?"

The sergeant ignores her, takes a deep breath and finally clicks the send button.

"Kilo Six," he mumbles. "Operation Clean Sweep is a go. Repeat: Operation Clean Sweep is a go." He closes his eyes tight and presses the radio against his forehead for a moment before continuing. "Sal, I'm bugging out. You're with me, right?"

The sergeant keeps his eyes tightly closed, as if he's silently praying until the response comes a few seconds later. "That's affirm, Alpha Niner. Will rendezvous at 5th and Prospect. Maintain radio silence. Out." He sighs with relief.

"Sergeant," I insist, "what the fuck is going on?"

The sergeant swings his rifle up to his shoulder, takes a brief look behind him at the closed door and starts to jog towards the trees, calling back over his shoulder. "If you want to live, follow me."

"What are you talking about?" I continue. "Hey, *stop*!"

The soldier doesn't break stride. "Come or stay, guys. It's all the same to me. I'm getting the hell out of here."

I turn to Kate and shrug my shoulders. "What the fuck? What do you wanna do?"

Kate chews her thumbnail for a moment, deep in thought. "I don't know," she finally replies, "but I think it might be a good idea to follow the guy with the gun."

I nod in agreement. Something about this sergeant rubs me the wrong way. I don't trust him as far as I can throw him, but the ashen look on his face makes me think that sticking around here to wait for help might be a bad career move.

"OK, sergeant, we're with you." We run to catch up with him as he vanishes into the trees, and both of us struggle to keep pace with his stride. "Now what the hell's going on?"

"What's going on, son," he says darkly, keeping up his steady pace, "is that an hour from now New York is going to have a sudden heatwave. Now keep up. There's a damned good reason I'm moving quickly."

****

Arnold sees the trees ahead of him. He's lost the trail. The sound stopped a while ago and he can't track down the source, but the gentle movement of the trees draws him in. Behind him the streets are silent and still. Ahead the branches sway and rustle in the breeze, and that's enough to urge him forward. Movement means life. Life means food.

He stumbles across a low chain blocking the entrance to the park, almost losing his footing, but he manages to plant his broken stump down on the other side and stay on his feet. He looks around. The others are still behind him. They don't seem quite as smart as he is. They move with less purpose, and they don't seem as driven. Maybe it's because Arnold has already taken lives. Maybe he's got more of a taste for it. Maybe he's just a little more hungry than the others. He doesn't know. Doesn't care.

He drags his ruined leg across the silent car park and out onto a patch of grass. Ahead of him he sees trees and bushes, but none of that interests him. His senses are tuned to something else, and something tells him he's not too far now. Soon he'll get to eat.

As he stumbles through the bushes and emerges onto a broad field of baseball diamonds a dim memory sparks in the slurry that used to be his mind. He remembers... something right on the edge of his memory, fighting its way through. Something about noise. Cheering. People. Right here. Something about this place means people. Maybe there are some still here, hiding somewhere.

He stumbles towards a row of white wooden bleachers. This is the place. This is where the people come, but there's nobody here. It doesn't make sense. This is where the people come, so why aren't they here?

The others behind him grunt impatiently. They want food, just like him. Where's the food? Where's the—

His head spins around at a sound carried on the shifting breeze. It's faint, but unmistakable. Voices.

The others pinpoint the source of the noise before he does, and they're already moving before Arnold sets off in a new direction. They all move north, more quickly now, towards a thick copse of trees.

People are somewhere on the other side. He's just sure of it.

He's excited.

****

"Operation Clean Sweep, that's what they call it." The sergeant shrugs his rifle to his shoulder and quickly vaults the low stone wall separating the park from Prospect Park West. I help Kate across and we jog to catch up with him. "Clean Sweep means we're royally fucked. It means we've lost control of the situation, kid."

"It's Tom," I say, scowling at him. "And this is Kate."

"Well, I'm Sergeant Laurence," he replies, his voice dripping with sarcasm, "and I'm positively *thrilled* to meet you. Now do you wanna stop and have a little tea party, or do you wanna shut the fuck up and let me explain?"

My fists ball up, but I manage to hold down my anger. "Fine. Go on."

"That's what I thought. OK, so we've got a pretty slim playbook for this kind of end of the world shit. We're not geared up for homeland defense on this scale, so we don't have many great options for a city like New

York. Our first and best hope was to blow the bridges, and use our—"

"Operation Pied Piper," Kate interrupts. "Yeah, we already heard about that." Laurence gives her a surprised look. "We came in with a firefighter who was involved in the planning," she explains. "He... he didn't make it."

"Right. OK, then you know Pied Piper was designed to cut off Manhattan and clear the city of hostiles. Maybe not completely, but enough to clear the way for ground forces and Operation Dragnet."

"Dragnet?" I ask. I haven't heard of that one.

"Sweep and clear. That was supposed to come next, once Pied Piper had taken out the bulk of the hostiles. Heavy ground forces would move south from the Bronx to secure and sanitize Manhattan one block at a time. Nothing fancy. Just slow, methodical work with well equipped and well armored infantry. Would have taken weeks for them to reach Battery Park, but it would have left the city intact and ready for reoccupation." He stops beside a parked Escalade on the corner where 5th Street meets the park, looks around and nods, satisfied there are no hostiles nearby. "OK, we wait here," he says, climbing up onto the hood for a better view of the street. "Sal will be along in five, then we get the fuck out of here."

"So, Dragnet," I say. "Sounds like a good plan to me."

Laurence snorts. "Yeah, it *was* a good plan, and it might have worked if luck had gone our way." He shakes his head and spits. "Whoever started this shit, they knew exactly how dumb we can be. See, all the scenarios we gamed out to retake the city, they were all based on the idea that the shit would start in one place. We thought they'd pick a crowded, central spot and infect hundreds of people at the same time. Thousands, maybe. Get a good swarm going."

"They didn't?" I ask, trying to hurry the story along.

"Uh uh. Now, I'm not far enough up the chain of command to know all the ins and outs, but I know a couple of guys in army intel who know the score. They said the NSA keeps constant surveillance on multiple key targets across the city. You know, Times Square, Central Park, most of the subway stations, that kind of thing. Since Bangkok they've been snooping on everything from police chatter to webcams to Instagram, watching out for anything that looks like an attack at those sites. They thought they could identify an outbreak within a few minutes and set things in motion before it had time to spread. They ran drills for this shit."

I pull my cigarettes from my pocket and offer them around. Kate shakes her head, and Laurence pulls one from the pack without thanking me. He plucks my Zippo from my hand and cups it against the breeze, taking a long pull before continuing, the cigarette bobbing up and down between his lips as he speaks. "I've no idea if the fuckers who did this knew we were watching for it, but they decided to kick it all off where we didn't have eyes. The first reports that came in were from places like, I don't know, Hoboken. Red Hook. Astoria." He blows out a cloud of smoke. "We were expecting it to start with a huge riot in Times Square, you know? Not with a couple of guys attacking a cab driver in Harlem at six on a Saturday morning. I don't know Harlem well, but I'm guessing that's not all that uncommon."

I light my cigarette and take a drag. "So you mean we were taken by surprise?"

"Surprise? Shit, there's an understatement. Forget five minutes, they didn't figure out what was going on for fucking hours. By the time they managed to get Pied Piper in place the infection had already spread. It was in Manhattan, Brooklyn, fucking Jersey City. Everywhere, man. Game over. All Pied Piper did was save *our* asses. It cleared out most of Brooklyn, so we get to sit here on this nice quiet street and enjoy a smoke, but shit... these things are everywhere else, and they're spreading further by the minute."

I can feel an icy shard in my chest. It's been there since I first heard the colonel on the radio, but now it's grown so large it feels like it's hard to breathe. I don't want to ask the obvious question. I don't really want to know the answer, but I know I have to.

"So... Operation Clean Sweep? That's what I think it is, right? They're gonna destroy Manhattan?"

Laurence nods. "Bingo, kid. Clean Sweep is the nuclear option." He sees my shocked expression. "Not *actual* nuclear. We're not dumb enough to nuke ourselves, it's just an expression. Right now six B-2 bombers are on the way from Whiteman AFB in Missouri, loaded with a fuckton of the latest in thermobaric ordnance. Those are fuel-air bombs, kid. Nasty fuckers. 500 yard blast radius, massive damage. An hour from now they'll raze the city to the ground and rip out the lungs of everyone from Yonkers to Newark. Trust me, we *don't* want to be around when those bombers arrive."

"Jesus," I mutter. I've read about fuel-air bombs, and I know there are few worse ways to— "Wait, *what*? Newark to Yonkers?"

Laurence nods. "Of course. We have to stop these fuckers spreading, and they're not just in Manhattan. We have to make sure we get every last one. I figure they'll try to cover a ten mile radius, so long as they have enough firepower."

"But what about everyone back in the park? We're just gonna let them die?" I look over at

Kate and see tears pricking her eyes. "There were *kids* back there, man."

"Hey, get off my back!" Laurence snaps. "I'm not dropping the damned bombs, am I? I didn't sign up for this shit. What do you want me to do, stick around and die with them out of solidarity? Sit in a nice little prayer circle and hope we fly right up to Heaven? Fuck that."

"We could at least warn them. Jesus, at least we could give them a fighting chance to get out before the bombs hit. How can we just leave them?"

Laurence sneers. "You really don't get it do you, kid? This is about survival of the *species,* boys and girls. This is it. If a few thousand uninfected have to die to make sure we hold that line it's a small price to pay. Hey look, our chariot awaits."

I follow Laurence's pointed finger south, where an enormous armored vehicle decked out in desert camouflage turns from a side street onto Prospect Park West. It's so wide it clips the wing mirrors of the parked cars, and I wince at the painful screech as its armored flank scrapes along the side of a panel truck sticking out too far into the road. The thing looks like a tank, apart from its eight huge wheels. As it draws closer I notice some kind of machine gun mounted to the roof.

"What the hell is *that*?" Kate asks, mouth agape.

Laurence slides down from the hood of the car. "That, my lady, is a Stryker Interim Armored Vehicle." He turns to us with a broad grin on his face. "She's beautiful, isn't she?"

The Stryker pulls up alongside us, and Laurence pats its side as he steps to the back. "Hop in, kids," he says, tugging open the rear hatch and climbing into the compartment. "For your safety please note the location of the emergency exits, which can be found here, here and here. We'll be cruising at an altitude of around six feet, and our flight time today will be however the fuck long it takes to clear the blast radius of several dozen face melting thermobaric explosives. You stewardess will circulate the cabin shortly with a variety of refreshments, and the in-flight movie will be the laugh a minute Bill Murray classic Groundhog Day."

Kate gratefully takes his hand and climbs into the rear compartment of the Stryker. I'm about to follow, but when I reach the door I freeze.

"This thing is... *Jesus*, Laurence, you could fit twenty people back here. And twenty more on the roof."

Laurence sighs angrily. "What's your point, kid?"

I step back from the vehicle and throw up my hands. "My point is that you could save three dozen of those poor bastards in the park. You don't even have to warn them all. Just grab a handful from the edge of the field and sneak them out. We have to go back!"

Laurence pinches the bridge of his nose as if he's coming down with a headache, and he squats down in the rear compartment to my head height. "Look, kid, I've done my two tours. See this leg?" He tugs up his right pant leg, and I'm shocked to see there's nothing there but a carbotanium shaft surrounded by black, calf-shaped muscular mesh. "This country has already taken its pound of flesh, with fucking interest. I've given five years and a leg to the service, and now it's time for Sergeant Laurence to get his dues, understand? I got my buddy, I got my Stryker, and I got my gun."

I feel the hairs stand up on my arms as he looks down at his rifle. A grin spreads across his face, and when he looks back at me his eyes are ice cold. "See, I was gonna be a nice guy about this. I thought you two seemed like nice enough kids, and I decided to do one last good deed before the world goes completely to shit, but you just had to get on my last nerve, didn't ya? You had to peck away and make old Sergeant Laurence feel like a bad guy just for looking out for himself." He levels his M16 at my face. "Well, you just lost your ticket to the fun bus, son. Now why don't you go ahead and take a few steps back?" I shuffle back, my eyes fixed on the barrel of the rifle pointing right at my eyes. "That's right, a little further. There's a good boy."

My throat feels like it's closed up with fear, but I manage to croak out a few words. "Kate, climb down."

Kate starts to move behind Laurence, but he holds out a hand to stop her. "*Ah ah ah*, stay right there, missy. Sal, you got her?" he calls out, keeping his eyes fixed on me.

"Uh huh, I got her," comes a voice from the front of the vehicle. I look behind Laurence and see a young Hispanic guy in fatigues, leaning back from the driver's seat with a pistol pointed towards Kate.

"Please, just let me go, OK?" Kate begs quietly, her voice quavering. "Just let me get out and you guys can leave. We won't make any trouble."

Laurence chuckles and shakes his head. "No, I think you'll be better off with us," he laughs. "I'm sure we can find some use for you."

My hands bunch into fists, and my heart pounds deafeningly in my ears. I've never felt this kind of pure, cold hatred towards another human being before. I want to beat him in the face with the butt of his own gun until I feel it hit the back of his skull. I want to pin him down under the wheels of his Stryker and drive slowly forward, waiting for the weight to squeeze his guts from his mouth like toothpaste from a tube. I want to watch him *burn*.

"Let her go, Laurence," I growl, my voice hoarse. "If you take her I'll hunt you down, and my face will be the last you ever see." Even I know how ridiculous my threat sounds, directed at a trained soldier pointing an M16 at my head from the back of his armored car. I've never felt more hatred, but I've also never felt weaker. I've never felt like such a worthless, powerless pussy, unable to so much as keep my girlfriend safe from harm. I feel like a little kid trying to stand up to a bully twice my size, jutting out my chin and puffing up my chest, knowing that the result will be a fist in the face and more humiliation.

Laurence bursts out laughing "Oh, you should see your face, kid," he chuckles, reaching out for the door handle. "Red as a fucking beetroot." He shakes his head and sighs happily. "Well, we gotta go, Liam Neeson. Enjoy the fireworks, y'hear?"

With that he starts to slam the door in my face, but through the gap I see Kate launch herself at the sergeant with murder in her eyes. The door swings back open as her head reaches the guy at stomach level, and the sergeant doubles over in pain as she winds him. I grab the door and climb up as the driver yells out, his pistol waving wildly. Kate scrambles up from the floor and kicks out at Laurence as I grab her and pull her back towards the hatch.

I don't register the shot. I know it's deafeningly loud in the enclosed space, but my ears just don't pick up the sound. All I see is a quick muzzle flash that lights up the dim cab for a moment, then I feel myself pushed backwards as Laurence kicks out at Kate's belly.

The two of us tumble out of the Stryker. I land first, cushioning Kate, and roll her off me onto the asphalt. The first thing I see is blood. Hers? Mine? I can't tell. It all happened too quickly.

"Kate? Kate, get up!" I lift myself to my feet and try to pull her from the ground, but she's limp in my hands. I tug again and her jacket falls open, exposing the white shirt beneath. A red patch spreads across her chest like a terrible Rorschach test. Her eyes are wide open, staring blankly at the sky. I stare at her lifeless body as a pool of blood gathers in the hollow of her throat and overflows, running in twin lines down both sides of her neck.

She's gone.

I barely notice the engine of the Stryker roaring back to life, and before I can react the vehicle suddenly reverses at speed straight towards me. I barely have time to blink before the protruding running board hits me in the stomach, forcing me to double over in pain, bringing my head down just in time to connect with a dull thump against a Jerry can mounted to the back.

The lights go out. I don't feel anything as my body is thrown back onto the road. I don't feel my back as it scrapes along the ground, and I don't feel my head thump against the asphalt. I feel nothing. I hear nothing. I see nothing. I don't see the tires run over Kate's lifeless body.

I don't even hear the screams as they draw ever closer.

****

For a moment my world is nothing but a high pitched tone and a distant point of light.

Slowly, bit by bit, my glazed, unfocused eyes open on the gray sky above, the dark clouds pinpricked with flashes of coloured light. My ears are ringing and I can hear each breath as a muffled roar in my head.

Suddenly the pain returns. Shocking. Sharp. I manage to turn my head before the vomit burns my throat, and I cough a spray of thin, milky puke across the black asphalt from the depths of my empty stomach.

The urge to sleep is almost overpowering. I'd like nothing more than to curl up on this asphalt bed and just take a moment to gather myself. Just a couple of minutes, I think, and then I'll be ready to move again. It's only the throbbing pain in the back of my head that keeps me from slipping away, an insistent jab of hot needles that forces my mind to wake. With a monumental effort I manage to raise myself onto my elbows, then force my body up into a seated position. I slump forward and puke again, this time between my legs. I cough again as it dribbles down my chin, spraying my pants and boots in clear vomit.

I reach gingerly to the back of my head, wincing at the sharp pain as I run my fingers through my hair. They come away bloody, but it's not quite as bad as I feared. I can't feel an open gash. Nothing that feels like it might need stitches. It just feels as if someone has taken a belt sander and gone to town on the back of my skull. The back of my head feels like a piece of tenderized meat, and my vision blurs as I stare at my bloodied fingers.

Apart from the throbbing pain in my head I feel... numb. Like I'm trapped in a dream. Everything about this just feels like it can't be real. I can't have woken up this morning to find the city overrun by insane, murderous creatures. I can't have beaten a man to death, and watched as another turned into one of those things. Most of all, I can't have just watched my girlfriend—

Oh.

Kate.

I look over at the lifeless body ten feet ahead of me. There's no question she's gone. The vehicle crushed her. I don't even want to look closer. I don't want that to be my memory of her. Not as a crushed, broken rag doll splayed on the ground in the middle of the street. I turn away and blink tears from my eyes.

This can't be real. It's ridiculous. Any minute now I'll wake up in my bed with Kate beside me, just another lazy Saturday with nothing to do but chill out in front of the TV and call in a pizza. It has to be a dream. *Just relax, Tom. Maybe it's OK to lay back down and just take a break for a little while. None of this is real. Why not just rest?*

Moments later reality hits me like a hammer. A sound I've been hearing subconsciously since I hit the ground finally forces its way through to my waking mind, and it shocks me awake in an instant, like a torrent of ice cold water to the face.

Screaming.

Thousands of voices, all of them screaming.

****

Arnold's excitement grows with each step. He can sense the mood in the group around him. They all sense it. They're all moving more quickly, and they know they're getting closer with each step.

The first of the group finally crests a small rise, and Arnold know their search is over the moment he sees the first one break into a run. He's lightning fast. Much faster than Arnold, struggling on his frustrating crumbled bony stump. He's moving slowly now, the spur of bone digging deep into the soft soil with each step, giving him a pronounced limp as he moves eagerly forward.

The moment he hears the first scream his limp is forgotten. Arnold finds fresh reserves of energy and breaks into a clumsy run as the first of them bursts out of the trees and into the crowd. The people scatter, terrified, but they can't move quickly enough in the crowd to escape.

Arnold doesn't pick a target. He simply throws himself into the tumult, reaching out with his good arm for anyone within grasping distance. They keep frustrating him, darting just out of reach as they scatter like a bait ball of swift, nimble sardines evading hunting tuna fish. He can't seem to move quickly enough with his ruined leg and his shattered shoulder throwing him off balance. He fears he'll never eat.

And then it happens. A woman runs blindly towards him, so focused on escaping the quicker creatures that she barrels right into him and takes them both to the ground. Arnold doesn't look a gift horse in the mouth. He sinks his teeth into her shoulder as they fall as one, and by the time they hit the grass he feels her blood gush down his throat and spray across his face. She screams frantically right in his ear, but the sound only excites him. It only makes him bite deeper.

Her delicious, exciting screams only last a few moments before they die away into bubbling, whimpering gasps. Arnold raises himself clumsily onto his hands and knees, twisting his head like a crocodile to tear a strip of warm, wet flesh from her neck. The woman convulses beneath him, and with a final breath she coughs hot blood in his face as he chews.

Beneath him he feels her body grow still. Her eyes, so full of terror, panic and pain just a brief moment ago, soften and lose focus, drifting from his face to stare glassily at the sky. He senses she's gone. Her meat is still attractive, but it's not perfect any more. Not quite as fresh and enticing as that of the people still fleeing. Why limit himself to just one body when there are so many to choose from?

He lifts himself slowly to his feet, still chewing his tasty treat as it begins to slide down his throat, and sets out towards the loudest screams. As he stumbles away on his broken peg leg he doesn't notice the woman begin to convulse once again. He neither knows nor cares what will happen to her, but a few minutes from now she'll be back on her feet and hunting alongside him. She won't remember his face. She won't realize he has a thick strip of her neck coiled inside his belly. She won't know anything, apart from the rage and endless hunger.

She certainly won't care about her luggage, an open suitcase spilling over with a dozen pairs of expensive shoes, nor the broken bodies of her husband and son laying beside it.

****

The noise is deafening. Terrifying. It's like standing in the bleachers at Yankee Stadium, only the cheers have been replaced with bloodcurdling screams.

But it isn't the volume that scares me. The screams pass over me like a wave, and a thousand are no more terrifying than a hundred. Quite the opposite. What scares me - what chills me to the bone - is that as the screams approach I can hear the cacophony grow steadily quieter. I can almost pick them out, one by one, as a voice falls silent, then another, and another. Maybe the people have simply lost the breath to scream. Maybe they've lost their throats. Neither thought is particularly comforting.

I hear the closest screams now, just on the other side of the park wall. Just beyond the trees, growing nearer by the second. I stand frozen, peering into the foliage, searching for movement, and it takes my concussed mind a moment to realize that the low park wall offers me no protection at all. I'm not a bystander here. I'm not impassively observing the situation like I'm watching the news on TV. These screams will reach me at any moment. They'll surround me and pass me, and the things that caused them will follow soon after.

I snap out of it and finally wake up. The fog lifts from my mind in an instant, and I hear my own voice above the screams. "You have to get out of here, Tom," I hiss to myself. "Go. *Now.*" I feel awful leaving Kate's body lying there like discarded trash but I know there's no other choice. My legs listen to my commands for the first time since the Stryker hit me and I launch myself into a clumsy, shambling run towards the intersection with 5th Street. My legs still feel like jelly and they send me careening straight into the side of a parked car on the other side of the street, but they at least propel me away from the screams and towards... it doesn't matter. *Away* is the only word that matters right now.

As I stumble onto 5th Street and start heading west I hear for the first time the groans and pants of the infected, loud enough to carry over the few screams that remain. The ungodly howls force my legs to move faster, launching me down the street at a speed I didn't know I was capable of attaining after almost three decades of junk food and sloth.

Behind me I can hear panting breaths, each one louder and closer than the last. Something is catching up fast, and I don't dare turn around to see if it's human or something else. I can't help but think of runners warning of the temptation to look back in the moments before crossing the finish line. Just a quick, momentary glance to see if there's anyone on their tail can be enough to make them fall behind; enough to cause them to break stride or stumble. For them the error could mean losing their lead by a nose, but for me it could mean death. I don't dare look back. I *can't*.

And yet... it keeps gaining, whatever it is. I won't allow myself the luxury of a panicked cry. I can't spare the breath. I scan the road ahead, searching desperately for some kind of escape route. I know my legs can't keep up this pace for much longer, and I can feel the bile rise in my throat again as my concussed, addled brain yells at me to stop and rest. It insists, firing warnings to my every muscle, forcing my vision down to a narrow tunnel and filling my ears with an insistent, sickening buzz.

My heart soars as I see the door of a townhouse swing open just a few car lengths ahead. For a moment I wonder if it's an hallucination. The bright red door seems to glow at the top of its stoop, beckoning me in to safety. It can't possibly be real, can it? Surely it's just a cruel joke played on me by my broken mind, tempting me to slow enough for the creatures to catch me. Enough for them to tackle me to the ground, climb up my body and sink their teeth into me as as I waste my final breath on a futile scream.

I've just about convinced myself it's a mirage. I've convinced myself it would be safer to keep running and hope I can outdistance the things chasing me, when a man steps out from the door and waves frantically, beckoning me towards him. I can see his lips move as he yells, but I've no idea what he's saying. Can't hear a word above the ringing in my ears. All I know is that he's undeniably *real*. I don't think my mind is sophisticated enough to hallucinate this fat, bearded guy, his stained white painter's overalls half hiding a T-shirt with a picture of Kevin Bacon's face constructed from strips of bacon.

I reach the stoop at a dead run and launch myself up the steps two at a time. That final explosive effort leaves me running on fumes and feeling as if the air is as thick as water. My legs finally give out as I hit the top of the stoop. They buckle beneath me, but the man saves me before I can stumble, reaching out to grab a fistful of jacket in his meaty hands. He lifts me bodily through the door, throwing me into the hallway beyond like a sack of potatoes before spinning on his heels and kicking it closed behind him.

As soon as the door slams closed, before I can even take my first ragged breath, the wood shakes in its frame as someone - some*thing* - slams against it. I can only assume it's one of the infected. It must have been the thing I could hear breathing, chasing just a few steps behind, and I'm amazed and relieved in equal measure that I managed to reach the door just a moment ahead of it. It must have been almost within grasping distance. Almost close enough to grab me by the clothes and pull me back. I shiver at the thought.

Then I hear the voice. Frantic. Pleading. Gasping. Begging to be let in. Whoever's on the other side of the door is *alive*. He hammers his fists against the heavy wood as he pleads. The man who rescued me rushes back towards the door and grabs the handle, and he's about to twist it when he freezes. The banging stops, suddenly replaced with an ear bleeding scream.

"Oh Lord, I thought he was chasing you," the guy cries, dropping to his knees and lifting the letterbox. "I thought he was one of *them*." He peers through the slit in the door, then immediately falls back in horror. I can only imagine what it is he sees, but I have a fairly good idea when he turns his haunted eyes towards me and raises a shaking finger to his lips. *Quiet.* There's nobody left to save on the other side. Not any more.

I take in my new surroundings as the man moves back to the letterbox and crosses himself. I'm in a long hallway, roughly decorated in the sort of Bohemian, artistic style that cost either fifty bucks or tens of thousands of dollars. I lean back against the curved leg of a wooden table covered in peeling paint and gasp with pain as my head nudges the corner of the tabletop. I forgot all about my head, but now the pain comes rushing back with a vengeance as the adrenaline begins to wear off. I reach to the back of my skull and find a lump that feels about the size of half a baseball bulging under my hair. Shit.

"Do you have a first aid kit?" I whisper, looking around the hallway as if I'll find a video game style medkit lying around.

"Me? Naw," he whispers, with a relaxed Southern drawl that would have seemed oddly out of place in Brooklyn even before its residents started eating each other. He turns away from the door and slides down to rest with his back against it. "This ain't my place, though. I was just here to paint the bedroom. You might wanna check the bathroom or something." He leans in towards me with a hopeful look. "Hey, don't suppose you got any cigarettes?"

I nod and fumble through my pockets for my pack, and when I pull out the box of Marlboros the guy's face lights up. "Thank the good Lord." He catches the pack and the

Zippo as I toss them over, and his hands shake as he gratefully slips one out. "I know this sounds shitty, but I pretty much only let you in to see if you had a smoke. Haven't had one all day, and I don't know about you but I really don't wanna go through the Rapture and the shakes on the same day." He takes a long drag, and looks up at the ceiling as he exhales. "Ah, that's the stuff. You can call me Bishop, by the way."

"Tom. Freeman. Look, Bishop, we need to get out of here right now."

Bishop gives me a look like I just suggested we climb to the roof and fly away. "No, no, no, no, *fuck* no. Are you crazy? There's no way I'm going out there. I got everything I need right here. Enough food in the kitchen to last 'til Christmas, and I've filled both bathtubs with water. This place'd be perfect if we had more cigarettes. We should just ride it out here until the cavalry rides in and sorts this shit out, y'understand?"

I shake my head. "There's no riding it out. The whole city's going to be flattened by the Air Force in less than an hour. Unless this place has a bomb shelter we need to get the fuck out of here right now. Please tell me you have a vehicle."

"OK, so we can hide downstairs, right? This place has a big old basement. Hell there's even a pool table down there."

"That's no good, Bishop." I look at his simple, vacant expression. I hate to make a snap judgment, but I'm not sure he'd be able to get his head around the idea that a basement would be no match for a fuel-air bomb exploding a couple of streets away. I barely understand the weapon myself, but I think talk of blast fronts and the fact that such a bomb could suck the oxygen right out of the building would just confuse him. Better to tell a simple white lie. "They're going to nuke the city. Now, do you have a car?"

"Jesus, it's that bad? Yeah, I got my truck right outside, but you don't wanna go out there. The street's full of those things. We wouldn't get two feet before they tore us up. Here, come take a look."

I pull myself to my feet and shuffle painfully across to the door. Every limb aches now, and I know I won't be able to push myself much further without medical attention and a fistful of painkillers. I crouch down and push open the flap of the letterbox, and my heart sinks when I see what's on the other side. Four infected fight over the remains of a body between the front door and the truck parked by the sidewalk, a beat up old red pickup with the words *F. Bishop Decorators* stenciled on the door.

"OK, we need to get them away from your truck. Do you have a gun?"

"Uh uh," his jowls swing back and forth as he shakes his head. "Couldn't get a carry permit from the city. I've got a bunch of paint brushes and a sandwich I brought from home. I didn't come tooled up for the end of the world, y'know? You can bet they're dealing with it better in the south, that's for sure."

"Fuck." I wonder for a moment if I should go searching the house for some kind of weapon, but I'm painfully aware that we're running out of time before the bombs drop. We need to be on the road in the next few minutes if we want to clear the blast radius.

"We need some kind of distraction. Something to draw them away."

Bishop scratches his beard, deep in thought. "Umm... I don't know, maybe one of us could run down the street and distract them while the other fetches the truck?"

Again I shake my head. "I'm pretty sure I'd pass out if I tried to run right now, and... look, I hate to be rude, but I'm pretty sure you're too heavy to outrun those things."

Bishop looks down at his hefty gut and nods glumly. "Oh wow. I never thought I'd get fat shamed during the apocalypse."

"Shit, sorry, I didn't mean to—"

"Nah, I'm just fucking with ya, man." He flashes a grin and takes a puff of his cigarette. "I think all that PC shit died when people started eating each other, right? You're right, though. A guy like me ain't worth shit in a foot race." He flinches as the burning tip of his cigarette drops into his lap. "Ow! Fuck!" he yelps, brushing the burning ash away.

A thought suddenly occurs to me as I watch the embers glow on his pants. "Wait a minute. You said you were a painter, right? You have all your gear inside?"

Bishop nods. "Yeah, it's all upstairs."

"You have chemicals? Paint thinner, stuff like that?"

"Yeah, some. Why?"

"Show me," I say, pulling myself painfully to my feet. "I think I have an idea."

****

I peer through the curtains of the living room window, scanning the street to make sure the infected by the truck aren't about to be joined by company.

"You think this'll work?" Bishop looks down at the bottle in his hand, holding it at arm's length as if he's afraid it might explode if he so much as breathes.

"Of course it'll work." I carefully pour the clear liquid into another glass Coke bottle, then tear a strip from my spare T-shirt to stuff in the neck. "Look, this is arson 101. You have nothing to worry about. Just watch what I do, OK?"

I stuff the rag into the neck of the bottle, then tip it on end until the gray rag darkens with soaked up liquid. "See what I'm doing? Get the rag good and wet with the acetone, then light it a couple of seconds before you toss it. Piece of cake. Understand?"

"Got it," he nods. "Umm... it's just, well, are you sure this is safe?"

I fill the third and final bottle, and stuff in the rag. "Bishop, I think at this juncture safety is very much a relative concept, don't you think?"

He frowns. "Huh?"

"Yeah, it's safe," I sigh, "so long as you don't drop it at your own feet."

Bishop still looks unsure. "Look, I don't want to say you're dumb or nothin', but see this label?" He picks up the plastic acetone bottle and points at the warning sign. "That means this stuff is explosive." He looks at me, and takes my blank expression for misunderstanding. "That means it might, y'know, blow up. You don't mess with this shit, understand? Are you sure you wanna set it on fire?"

I take the bottle out of his hand. "Bishop, look out the window. Look at those things in the street. Now look at this warning label and tell me what you're more afraid of." I set the bottle down on the windowsill beside the three Molotov cocktails. "The time for warning labels is over, know what I'm saying? Now look, don't worry about this stuff. I'll toss it out. You go look out the letterbox, and as soon as they move away from the truck sneak out and get ready to drive, OK?"

Bishop smiles, relieved, as if he thinks he's been given the safer job. "OK, sure, I can do that. You gotta hurry though, OK? I don't want to wait around for you out there."

"I'll be right on your heels, trust me." I glance at my watch. "I think we have about a half hour to get clear. OK, go on now. Good luck, Bishop."

The lumbering giant takes a deep breath then heads out to the hallway with a nervous look on his face. I turn back to the window, push it open as quietly as I can and pick up the first of the bottles. The acetone has already evaporated from the rag, so I tip the bottle upside down again until it darkens once more.

The wheel of the Zippo lighter sounds far too loud as I strike it, and I freeze for a moment as one of the infected outside looks up from his meal and casts his eyes around the street. He looks like he heard me, but I have no time to worry about it now. I hold the flame to the rag and flinch as it catches with a soft *woomph* and a pall of greasy smoke, and I slowly, carefully lean out the window and toss the flaming bottle with a slow, swinging underarm throw as far as I can down the street.

It lands with a dull thump around twenty yards away, in a little gated patch of grass beside a stoop three doors down. I can barely see it from the window, but it looks like the flame went out before it landed. *Shit*. Maybe the acetone isn't flammable enough?

I grab the second bottle and tip it on end, holding it upside down even longer this time, soaking the rag until it starts to drip onto the floor. Again I light the rag, and this time the fire is much more excitable. I lean out the window and toss it high up into the air and right in the middle of the street. I pray as it sails in a graceful arc and thank God as the bottle shatters on the asphalt, the sound echoing between the houses. The mob of infected look up as one at the pool of fire spreading in the middle of the road.

Their excitement is immediately obvious.
Three of the group sprint at full speed
towards the flame, and when they reach it
they circle, confused, unsure whether it's
something to be attacked.

But there's a problem. The fourth creature is
still hunched over the body by the truck,
facing away from the flames and oblivious to
the excitement, and now his cohort has
gotten out of the way I see why. The side of
his face I can see is almost completely gone,
eaten away. Even from this distance I can see
his exposed jaw move as he uselessly chews,
the meat falling out of his mouth as soon as
he scoops it in. Where his ear once was is
now just a pink, pulpy mass of blood and
matted hair. He must be half deaf, and
couldn't hear the bottle shatter.

My mind races as I try to think of a solution.
Maybe I could toss the bottle a little closer to
him in the hope that his other ear is good, but
that might only draw the others back towards
the truck. Maybe if I—

I freeze at the sound of the front door
creaking open. I lean out the window and
almost call out when I see Bishop step

outside. He walks as if he's trying to be stealthy, but for someone that large it would be impossible. Even from here at the window I can hear each footstep as he treads down the steps.

The three infected at the fire seem oblivious, still entranced by the dancing flames, but I know the fourth will launch himself at Bishop the moment he sees him. There's just no way the guy can get into the truck without being detected, and his hands are empty apart from the keys. He doesn't even have a stick to fend it off.

There's nothing for it. I know it's a terrible plan but I grab the final Molotov cocktail and tip it up, soaking the rag. I only have a few seconds before Bishop is fucked. I light it with a *woomph* then toss it as precisely as I can, aiming for a spot just in front of the truck, within the creature's eyeline but out of view of the others.

As the bottle sails through the air my heart sinks. The flame goes out almost as soon as it leaves my hand, and it's wildly off target. In the time it takes to complete its arc I picture what will come next in my head. The bottle will shatter on the street, and all four infected will look up and see the big, lumbering oaf Bishop standing there with nothing but his dick in his hand. They'll tear him apart before he can take so much as a slow, leaden step, and he'll go to the grave with the truck keys. All that will be left for me is to find out whether I'll die in a fiery explosion or get torn apart by those fuckers outside running in through the wide open front door.

My mind is running so fast I barely notice the speed with which Bishop moves. Everything seems to move in slow motion as he sees the bottle, reaches out and scoops it from the air moments before it hits the asphalt, gripping it by the neck with his meaty fist. I don't dare breathe as I watch, amazed, as he brings the base of the bottle down on the back of the creature's head like he's stamping a library book. It doesn't even shatter. It just sends the thing silently sprawling to the ground with a knockout blow. Bishop turns slowly to the window, gives a cheery wave and flashes me the most shit-eating grin I've ever seen.

I don't waste any time. Already the fire down the street is dying, and I know as soon as Bishop starts the engine the three remaining infected will notice him. I limp as quickly as I can through the house, ignoring the pain radiating through my body, and reach the front door just in time to watch Bishop fire up the engine and fishtail out into the street with the squeal of spinning wheels.

"You *fuck*!" I yell after him, feeling the dull, impotent certainty that my last chance at survival is tearing away faster than I could ever hope to run. "You rotten fucking *cunt*!" I know there's no way to catch him, but I need to try anyway. I can't just stand here and wait for the end to come. If I die I'll die running, dreaming of what I'd do to that fat, cowardly prick if I ever caught up with him.

I almost fall down the steps in my rush to reach the street, swearing under my breath. The three infected have already begun to sprint towards me, and it's all I can do to force my legs to obey my commands. I break into a run knowing that every step is futile. I can't outpace them, and I sure as hell can't outdistance them. Even if I could I'd never make it out in time before the—

I hear a squeal at the end of the street, the tortured revving of an engine, and I almost can't believe what I'm seeing as I emerge from between the parked cars and get a clear look down the street.

The pickup barrels back down the street towards me, frighteningly quick, and in the moment before it reaches me I see Bishop's grinning face as clear as day through the windscreen. He speeds past me so close that I feel my jacket shift in the turbulence and I spin around just in time to see the truck mow down the three infected, scattering two of them like bowling pins and sending the third beneath the wheels. The truck bounces over it, crushing it to a pulp and leaving the thing sprawled in the middle of the street, twitching its shattered limbs and silently moving its jaw as if trying to bite the memory of the tires.

The truck cruises to a halt, and I see Bishop turn in his seat and look through the rear window as he shifts it into reverse. He drives backwards at speed, aiming for the broken creature, and this time shatters its skull beneath the wheels before bouncing off it and pulling to a stop beside me.

"Woo, what a *rush*!" Bishop grins like an overexcited kid and leans over to push open the passenger door. "Well, you waiting for a red carpet, your majesty? Come on, get in."

I don't say a word as I climb in the car and buckle up. I don't speak as Bishop shifts back into drive and bounces over the pulped body of the creature a final time. I only manage to catch my breath long enough to direct him south to the Verrazano bridge. My heart pounds in my throat, and my vision narrows to a pinpoint as unconsciousness finally overtakes me.

Fucking Bishop.

****

I dream.

I dream the story told to me by Paul McQueen, my old friend back in Bangkok. I'm standing above the street, watching the terrified crowd turn. Searching for Kate in the chaos, hoping - *praying* - I'll find her in time to pull her away from the grasping hands trying to pull her down with them to hell.

There she is. I see her hiding from the violence by the side of the street, a solitary blonde head in amongst the dark haired crowd. I yell out to her at the top of my lungs, begging her to run, but my voice emerges as nothing more than a whisper. She can't hear me above the crowd. Doesn't even look my way. She's staring open mouthed at the horror around her. Teeth tearing into flesh. Fingers forcing their way into wounds, tearing them wide open as the victims scream. The street is awash with blood, flowing into every crack in the sidewalk. Filling the gutters until they overflow.

I try to run towards her, down to the street to pull her away to safety, but it feels as if I'm wading through molasses. I can't make any headway, and the crowd is only growing more frantic by the second.

Then I see him, standing between me and Kate, blocking the stairway down to the street. Sergeant Laurence. He towers over me, eight feet tall and grinning as he spots me. Blood drips from his smiling lips and runs down his chin and he chews a mouthful of flesh. My feet stick to the ground as if they're buried in cement. I can't move a muscle, even as Laurence charges towards me.

He tackles me by the waist and pushes me to the ground, pinning me down. I can't fight back. Can't even get in a punch as he begins to pummel me. I open my mouth to scream as he leans down over my prone body, but nothing emerges even as his hands reach into my mouth, one gripping each row of teeth, and he pulls my jaw wide open until the skin of my cheeks stretches so much it begins to tear.

Then... a bright light. Blinding. A sound like a freight train in my ears, overwhelming my senses until I can't even feel the pain any more. I close my eyes tight but the brightness doesn't diminish. I manage to raise my hands to my ears but the sound doesn't fade. It only grows louder, and louder still.

"Tom." I barely hear the voice above the roar.

"Tom." A little louder now, breaking through. I open my eyes just in time to see Kate standing above me, a silhouette against the blinding light.

"*Tom*!"

The sky falls away below me as I open my eyes. I see two suns set at once, one behind me, red, muted and hidden in haze, the other ahead, blindingly bright, impossibly large and close. Just a few feet away I see fire hanging down from above, the fierce flames swept towards me by the wind.

It takes my mind a moment to figure out what I'm looking at. I'm upside down, pinned to my seat by the belt that digs into my shoulder and cuts deeper into my skin with each breath.

I'm still not fully awake. I feel like I'm sitting safely in the back of my own head, watching my life roll by dispassionately on a screen. I look up, craning my neck to the ceiling, and see a shallow pool of blood gather in the creases of dented bare steel. Another drop splashes into the pool as I watch, and I smile at the hypnotic sight of the liquid rising from my head and levitating its way to the ceiling until it hits the pool and sends a ripple across the surface. For a moment I try to figure out the trick. How did they manage to make the blood weightless?

Oh yeah. Upside down. Huh.

It's the next explosion that finally tugs me back to the world. Through the cracked windscreen I watch as a black plane drops something, then banks and gains altitude as the falling object sprouts a parachute. It's weird to watch it upside down. It looks like the plane is sailing across a cloud sea, firing its payload high into the sky.

The rumbling of the jet finally reaches me as the parachute nears the ground, but I can't see it any more. It's vanished from my narrow little window on the world, and the thing it dropped falls slowly, gracefully, its silence in counterpoint to the roar of the jet. From my point of view the parachute looks like it's rising slowly into the air, like a balloon that slipped from a child's hand.

The first silent burst makes me flinch in my seat and wince as the belt cuts deeper. It pops silently in a gray cloud, like a monochrome firework, and my mouth gapes open as the gray burst suddenly erupts, a fraction of a second later, in a blinding flash of light, darkening to a deep orange. It's...

I've never seen anything quite so beautiful. I can't tear my eyes away from the—

The shockwave hits me like a punch to the gut, forcing the air from my lungs. Colored spots appear in my eyes as I struggle for breath, and just a second later the noise reaches me, deafeningly loud. Distant car alarms begin to sound, and somewhere far behind me dogs howl, startled by the noise of the blast.

My mind clears in an instant, and with it the pain returns with full force. I reach up to my side and fumble for a moment until I find the seatbelt release, and I press the button without thinking. I fall hard, landing headfirst in the pool of blood gathered above me, and I scramble quickly through the broken window, my palms digging into shards of shattered safety glass strewn like gravel across the ground.

"Bishop," I call, my voice hoarse and low. "*Bishop*!" I feel like I've swallowed a bag of sand, my throat hurts so much.

As my vision clears I lay on my hands and knees and stare, confused at the scene around me. On either side of the road great steel rods climb high into the air like the bars of a giant's prison cell. Out in front an enormous archway towers over me, the road leading beneath it and on towards the setting sun, away from the artificial sun burning bright in the opposite direction.

It's only after a few moments of confusion that I realize I'm on the Verrazano Bridge, a couple of hundred yards from the Staten Island shore. I haven't crossed the bridge in years - nobody goes to Staten Island without a damned good reason - but I've seen it in the distance often enough to recognize the shape.

Ahead of me the world looks perfectly normal, just as it did yesterday. The sun sets on another lazy spring Saturday in America. Tomorrow it will rise like always to light gardeners tending their yards, golfers perfecting their swing on pristine, overpriced courses, moms cooking and freezing next week's gluten free, low carb meals, bored kids firing racist slurs through their gaming headsets, and everything else people do with their Sundays.

Behind me...

Behind me life will never be the same again for those few who managed to get out. I turn back to look at the Long Island shore and see nothing but destruction. A thick, greasy pall of black smoke climbs high in the sky and spreads as far as the eye can see, hiding the bare, bleached bones of my city. Buildings are flattened right up to the shore parkway, and more collapse as I watch. The smell reaches me, carried on the breeze. It's indescribable. *Everything* burning, all at once. Wood. Tires. Trees. Gasoline. Plastic.

People.

My mind can't possibly grasp the extent of the destruction. It's just too big to fit in one head. I can stare at the ruins, but I can't make myself believe that somewhere hidden beneath that shroud of smoke my apartment has been blown apart by an unimaginable force, and everything in it scattered to the wind. My clothes. My ATM cards. My passport, laptop, cameras, the half finished memoir I've spent the last year of my life writing, and every photo I ever took. I can't believe that my parents' house in Queens is gone, following the path they themselves took years ago. Somewhere in the smoldering wreckage their bones are buried, six feet beneath the ground in a cemetery within a cemetery.

My old high school is gone, and the playground where I had my first kiss with Tammy DiMicco. The dank, smoky little bar on Doughty Street where I once got an awkward handjob in the restroom from a middle aged woman who wore rings on all her fingers. The humid little bodega where I buy my cigarettes, always filled with a strange, overpowering spicy smell I could never quite place. All gone.

And then there's Manhattan itself.

I can't even think about that right now. It's too much. Too big. Its destruction belongs in movie theaters and nightmares, not the real world.

I look north, and for a moment - just a brief, beautiful moment - I manage to forget the destruction. Far off in the distance, almost too small to see and hidden beneath the smoke, a familiar sight stands tall. Marooned in the middle of the upper bay, briefly caught in the light of the setting sun, the Statue of Liberty rises high above the black water.

"At least you made it, girl," I whisper. I know it's dumb, but I feel comforted that some remnant of the city I've called home for almost thirty years still stands. Even if everything else has been wiped from the earth and ground into the dirt, at least she's still there to mark the grave on the map.

Here Lies New York City.

****

A half mile away at the Long Island shore a high pitched hum pervades the air, just at the edge of hearing, if there was anyone left alive to hear. Above the crackle of fires and the creak of settling concrete the hum grows louder by the second. It's the sound of straining. Of tension.

If anyone was around to see they might hear the occasional tortured *twang*, like the snap of an immense guitar string. If they were paying close attention they may just notice, in the heavy concrete anchorage of the bridge's main suspension cables, hairline cracks appearing in the concrete, weakened by the force of the blasts.

****

"Tom?" The weak voice carries above the breeze whistling through the cables. "Tom, are you there?"

My eyes dart around, searching for the source of the voice. "Bishop? Bishop, is that you?"

"Over here, buddy. Under the truck."

I turn back to the overturned pickup and fall to the ground, peering beneath the wreckage. I see him immediately, his pudgy face smiling weakly out from the narrow gap between the asphalt and the mangled bed of the truck.

"I see you, Bishop." I run over to the truck and crouch down to look through the gap. "Jesus, how did you get under there?"

"I don't rightly remember, buddy," he laughs, then loses his breath and descends into a coughing fit in the dusty air. "I guess I should have been wearing my seatbelt," he mumbles, his voice dry and scratchy. "I just looked around when I heard the first bombs, then it all kinda went to shit. I think I must have hit a barrier or something, 'cause next thing I know I'm out of the truck and all I can see is sky. I'm sorry, Tom, I fucked up. You OK?"

I nod and wave my hand. "Yeah, yeah, don't worry about me, I'm good. Just a few scratches."

Bishop twists his head so he can look out at me, and he winces when he sees my face. "That don't look like a scratch, Tom. You're redder'n a strawberry."

I reach up and touch my forehead, and my hand comes away sticky. "Don't worry about it," I assure him, "head wounds always look worse that they are. Now, we gotta get you out from under there. Can you move?"

Bishop wriggles a little beneath the truck, and nods. "Yeah, thank God. Don't seem to be caught under anything. Lucky escape, huh?"

"I think someone's looking out for you, Bishop," I laugh. "If you were anyone else you'd have already died three times today.

Now, we need to lift this thing somehow. I don't think you can squeeze through this gap."

Bishop shakes his belly with his hands. "I knew I shoulda started that diet at New Year. Couple less pizzas and I might have been able to fit. Hang on, I think I can squeeze through if you can just lift it a few more inches."

I move around to the back of the truck and grip the tailgate, but as much as I strain to lift it the truck won't budge. I try again, pulling up until I feel bile rising in my throat and see spots in my eyes, but I can only manage to move it an inch or so before my strength runs out.

"No dice, Bishop," I gasp. "I need some kind of leverage to get this fucker off the ground. It's just too heavy for me."

Bishop bangs his head against the asphalt, frustrated. I crouch back down to see if I can figure out another approach, but it doesn't look good. His body fills most of the space beneath the overturned flat bed. The base of it is just an inch or two from his protruding belly, too low for him to use his arms or legs to offer any help. The only other thing under there is...

"Bishop?" I ask slowly, almost afraid to finish the thought. "What's that thing next to you?"

He turns his head to the squat red canister strapped into a housing in the bed of the truck. It's about the size of a gas bottle for a camp stove, and so dirty I can't quite be sure if it is what I think it is.

"That's the, umm, bottle jack," he says, as if I just asked him to identify a bird that just flew by.

"Bishop..."

He gives me a blank look. "Yeah?"

"You wanna pass me the damned jack so I can lift the car and get you the fuck out from under there?"

The light appears in Bishop's eyes as he finally understands. I wonder if he's always this slow, or if he's just suffering from some kind of shock from the events of the day. He twists awkwardly in place and stretches his arm out until he can just about scrabble at the strap, loosening it with his fingers.

The hum reaches me before the vibration. For a moment I think it's just the same ringing that's been in my ears all day. I think it's just a symptom of stress, or something to do with the fact that I haven't had a bite to eat or a sip to drink since last night, paired with a couple of nasty head wounds.

But then I feel the road wobble.

It would be difficult to describe it to anyone who hasn't felt a good sized earthquake. It's not like the road is visibly bucking beneath me. It's just a tremble, easily ignored if I wasn't paying attention, but I can feel it all the way up my legs. Something's happening, and my Spidey sense starts tingling.

"Bishop," I say, trying to keep my voice calm, "maybe you should hurry up and get me that jack. Come on now, get it moving."

"I can't quite..." He bears his teeth and tries to stretch further, but he's at his limit. The thick strap is loosening, but only by a fraction of an inch with each tug. At this rate it'll take forever. I drop to my belly and shuffle as far as I can beneath the truck, and with a little effort manage to reach my hand out to loosen the thing with a quick tug.

I feel the vibration in my stomach as I slide the jack out from under the car. I can't be sure, but it seems to be growing stronger, quickly, and every few seconds I'm certain I can feel a slight jolt. I just pray it's in my head.

"OK, man, get ready to slide yourself out as soon as it starts to lift." I search for a decent jacking point at the bent lip of the flatbed. There's no spot I'd choose in a perfect world, but the nearside corner seems solid enough for the job at a pinch. I plant the bottle firmly on the asphalt beneath the steel, and with shaking hands insert the collapsible lever and start pumping. The piston creeps up painfully slowly, and by the time it finally connects with the steel the hum in the air has shifted to a distant, tortured squeal.

"Hear that noise, Bishop?" I try to keep the growing panic from my voice, without much success.

"You too? I was hoping I was just going crazy." I hear the exact same scared tone echoed in his voice. "That... that's not a good sound, is it?"

I'm pumping frantically now, raising the truck achingly slowly, a fraction of an inch at a time. "No, that's not a good sound. I think the bridge might be coming down. You think you can start to move?"

"Just a couple more inches and I think I'll be able to— what the *fuck* is that?"

****

Back at the shoreline the tortured cable finally gives way at the south anchorage point. With the sound of a thousand gunshots the cable snaps loose from the concrete, whipping out across the roadway and tearing the vertical suspension cables from their moorings. In just a few seconds the unsupported deck begins to tilt down like a swinging trapdoor, held in place only by the single remaining main cable. A wave ripples down the length of the bridge at breakneck speed as the entire section of deck before the first tower crumbles away and collapses into the water below.

****

Bishop wriggles frantically out from beneath the truck, scraping his ass across the glass-strewn asphalt without a care for the pain. I look back towards Long Island and see the main cable catapult into the air. At this distance it appears as slender as gossamer, but I know I'm watching a couple hundred yards of three foot thick steel spring high into the sky like it's weightless. When the sound reaches me I immediately abandon the jack. There's no time to raise the truck higher. I run around to the side and grab Bishop by the scruff of his neck, leaning back and dragging with all my might to tug his weight clear. He twists and struggles in my grip, fighting to free himself, and the moment his feet clear the truck the road bucks and rolls wildly. The jack tips and the back of the truck collapses, closing on the asphalt like a bear trap.

"Come on!" I yell, pulling Bishop to his feet. "We gotta get the fuck out of here!"

He doesn't need any more encouragement. As we start to run we both hear the tortured snaps as each vertical cable in turn breaks under the load, unable to support the weight of the deck without the help of the broken cables before it. I'm running as fast as my legs will carry me, but if I could see the chain reaction catching up with us my legs would be a blur.

****

The trembling deck of the bridge collapses piece by piece, dropping a twenty yard section at a time into the frigid black water of the Narrows. The vertical support cables snap from their moorings like cut tendons, springing upwards with the release of tension. The deck beneath each broken section tilts, listing towards the south, straining on the opposite cables until they too collapse under the strain, sending the deck tumbling down into the churning waters below.

The collapse only accelerates as ever more cables fail. The first few sections fell slowly, holding the strain for several seconds before plummeting, but now they fall like a row of dominoes as each remaining section strains under the weight, not only of itself but of the thick, heavy cable sinking to the bottom of the Narrows.

****

The noise is deafening now. Each tumbling section adds yet more force to a rumble I can feel resonate through my body. It's barely even sound any more. It's so loud it's become almost a physical presence surrounding me. Beneath my feet the deck of the bridge shakes so much I feel like I'm trying to run across the surface of a bounce house. My knees buckle with every step, and beside me Bishop is doing no better.

"We're almost there!" he yells above the roar, pointing towards the tall gray archway on which the suspension cables rest. It's less than fifty yards ahead of us, and Bishop believes that's the finish line.

I know better. I wish I didn't.

A few years ago, stuck in a cramped aisle seat on a late night Aeroflot flight from Ulaanbaatar to Moscow, I found myself so bored that I spent an hour watching a Russian language documentary about marvels of engineering. I drifted in and out for most of it, but I remember paying close attention when a simulation of a bridge collapse showed up on screen. The image creeps back to the front of my mind now, bringing me little comfort as it dredges up half forgotten facts I'd set aside as useless as soon as I heard them, never imagining it would ever matter to know exactly how a suspension bridge works.

The fact is that reaching the tower won't ensure our safety. Nowhere near, in fact. Beyond the tower there's at least two hundred yards of bridge remaining before it ends in the cable anchorage, and that means there's at least two hundred yards of three foot thick, immensely heavy cable on that side of the tower. I look up, and wish I hadn't. I see four cables, two on each side, along with at least a couple of dozen vertical support cables holding up the bridge. Once the bridge collapses as far as the tower all those cables will go slack, sending the rest of the bridge to the bottom of the Narrows. The cables don't just hold up the center span of the bridge. They hold up the whole thing, all the way back to shore.

No, the only safe place here - and 'safe' is hardly the word - is the tower itself. The tower is the only part of the bridge that's properly grounded, and can stand without the support of the cables. Once this is over there's at least a slim chance it will still be standing.

Bishop tries to accelerate ahead of me, panicking at the sound of approaching collapse. I don't dare look behind to see how close it is, but I know running beyond the tower won't help. We need to find— ah, there it is.

"Bishop!" My voice barely carries over the noise, and he only hears me on the second attempt. "Follow me!" I turn towards the north edge of the deck, terrified that the next big shake will flip me over the edge, but I know there's no choice. The edge is where the only hope of salvation lies.

We finally reach the tower, and I vault clumsily over a railing onto a steel grated walkway probably built for service staff. Through the grating I can see the lower deck of the bridge, surrounded by the thick steel support structure that I'd swear could withstand an asteroid strike if I hadn't already seen it torn apart like wet tissue paper. I feel the grating rattle as Bishop lifts his bulk over and I grip the railing, suddenly afraid that his weight might be the straw that breaks the camel's back.

I don't even try to yell this time. The noise is just overwhelming, and I can see the collapse is only fifty yards from us. I grab Bishop by his collar and point to the steel stairwell running around the outside of the tower, heading down towards the lower deck. I don't wait to see if he understands. I just run.

The steel rattles wildly as the deck collapses around it. I grab hold of the railing for dear life, and my stomach flips over as I feel the stairway break away from the concrete wall. All around me the deck of the bridge tumbles away down to the water far below, and I just cling to the railing and squeeze my eyes closed, praying to be saved by a God I don't believe exists.

The torture goes on for another minute before the noise finally fades. The sound of shattering concrete and rending steel was so loud that its absence sounds even louder. As the last of the bridge hits the water the silence that returns sounds deafening. Alien. Bizarre.

I risk opening my eyes, and when I see where I am my knuckles whiten on the steel railing. The staircase is at least ten feet from the wall of the tower, disconnected at the top and hanging on at the bottom by just a few bolts driven into the concrete.

"Bishop?" My whisper sounds like a yell in the sudden quiet.

"Yep?" The voice comes back muffled, and I look over to find Bishop with his arms wrapped around a steel bar, his face buried in his chest to avoid having to look at the ground fifty yards below.

"You still alive?"

"I don't know." He finally looks up at me and wrinkles his nose. "Does heaven smell like people who've shit their pants?"

I manage a soft laugh. "I don't think so, buddy."

"In that case I'm probably alive. And I need a bath."

"Do you think you can work your way down to—" The staircase creaks ominously, and my heart skips a beat at the sound of a bolt pinging from the concrete. "Move, Bishop, *now.*" I try not to sound panicked, but there's no concealing it. I can feel the staircase swing in the breeze, and I know it won't support our weight much longer.

Bishop reaches the foot of the staircase first, sliding across the steel on his belly like a snake, moving nervously from one section of railing to the next. I follow quickly behind, and when I catch up I find him frozen in place, unwilling to cross the yard wide gap between the foot of the stairs and the thick support girder still firmly fixed to the tower.

"Come on, man, you have to climb over there. This thing's gonna fall any second now, understand?"

He clings to the final railing and looks back at me, shaking his head with tears in his eyes. "I can't. I've got a thing about heights, Tom. I can't move."

"Bishop, you have no choice. If you don't get out of the way I can't get across. Either move now or we'll both die. *Move*!"

His mouth just opens and closes silently, and he shakes his head once more. I can see every tendon in his chubby hands picked out like taut violin strings as he clings onto the railing for dear life. There's nothing for it. I reach forward, stick my hand between his legs and squeeze his balls until he cries out in agony. He lets go of the railing and brings his hands down to protect himself, and I yell as loud as I can. "*Goooooo*!"

By some miracle it works. He's so distracted by the pain he scrambles to his feet and steps across the gap onto the girder, sending the staircase shaking loose as he goes. I shuffle forward as he drops down to hug the steel, and just as I stand to step across the chasm I feel the world give way beneath me.

Time seems to slow to a crawl. It's a strange feeling. My stomach flutters as the support beneath my feet simply stops being there, and for a moment it feels as if the world has forgotten about the laws of gravity. I hang unsupported in mid air, a gap of air between my feet and the rapidly accelerating staircase, and I feel a strange, brief rush of dizzying elation before time comes rushing back with a vengeance. Gravity returns, and I feel the ground far below sucking at my feet, pulling me down to meet it. The last thought that passes through my mind as I begin to fall is simple:

What the fuck is that?

And then I feel myself yanked to a halt. I look up and find myself safe in the meaty grip of a bizarre angel. An angel with a mullet, a scruffy beard and a T-shirt with Kevin Bacon's face painted in bacon strips.

Bishop strains with my weight, shifting himself on the girder to steady me. "Promise me one thing, Tom," he growls, "or I swear to the Lord God I'll let you fall." He takes a deep breath and lets out an angry sigh. "You will *never* touch my balls again unless I damn well ask you to. Is there an understanding between us?"

I can feel my sanity slipping away. Maybe it's the height. Maybe it's the fact that I just watched a bridge collapse around me. Maybe it's the sight I just saw far below. For whatever reason I can't help myself break into a fit of the giggles. I can barely catch my breath, but I finally manage to get it out. "It's a deal. Pull me up."

Bishop lifts me easily with one arm, depositing me on the wide girder where I lean over and hug it for dear life, terrified that I'll laugh so much I'll fall off.

"What's so God damned funny?" Bishop demands, holding a hand over his balls and scowling at me.

"Look down, Bishop. Look at the water," I manage, gasping for air. "Tell me God isn't fucking with us."

Bishop peers nervously over the edge of the girder and finally sees why I've lost it.

Fifty yards below us thousands of tons of shattered concrete, steel supports and the few cars that remained on the bridge have plunged to the depths of the Narrows. Most of the wreckage sank straight to the bottom, but on the way it hit something that doesn't belong.

It hit a net.

Fifty yards beneath us the black, cold water of the Narrows churns and froths like a scene from the end of Titanic. In the darkness countless infected thrash about in the water. Many are tangled in the remains of the net. Many more were crushed by the falling bridge and buried beneath tons of concrete on the riverbed. I look downriver, and in the fading light I see the churning white foam kicked up by thousands of struggling bodies. Thousands of infected floating freely, released from their prison. Many of them will be carried out by the current, I'm sure. Many of them will bloat and rot far out to sea, without ever setting foot on land again.

But some of them won't. In the dim light I can already see dozens of bodies struggle from the water. Maybe hundreds, dragging themselves to shore like rats.

Bishop plants his forehead on the cold steel girder and closes his eyes. "It's not over, is it?"

I shake my head and watch the land. The power is still running on Staten Island, and as the automatic street lights flicker on street by street they cast their glow on the heaving, wriggling shore, the narrow beach hidden beneath the dark crowds of infected crawling to land.

No, Bishop." My laughter has gone now. "I think this may just be the beginning."

****

The sight of guns is comforting. We're in the back of a covered truck with an armed soldier - a real soldier, not a terrified cadet like Karl, or a sociopathic asshole like Sergeant Laurence - speaking into his radio in incomprehensible military lingo as the truck rumbles down the deserted highway. The sound of radio chatter almost lulls me to sleep, but Bishop nudges me in the side and mutters a few words to make sure I stay awake.

The medic shined a bright light in my eyes when we dragged our dripping bodies up the shore and found the military roadblock at the bridge toll booths, and he warned me that I probably have a concussion. He poured an irresponsibly large pile of Tylenol into my hands and told Bishop to keep me awake until we reached the camp.

I warned the soldiers at the roadblock about the infected reaching shore, and felt a weight lift from my mind as they assured me they had the situation under control. A 'mop-up crew' was working its way along the shore, taking out anything that moved. In fact, they told us, they were about to open fire on us until Bishop yelled at them as we approached.

I wouldn't have blamed them. Bishop looked half OK, but it would be hard to guess I wasn't infected at a glance. I caught sight of my reflection in the window of a toll booth, and if I was armed I'd have pulled the trigger without a second thought. My face was covered with blood, and my hair was plastered to my head. I barely recognized myself, but even if I'd been clean I would have noticed the difference.

It's in the eyes. I noticed them as soon as I saw my reflection. I've seen those eyes once before, looking out at me over a cold bottle of Singha at a rickety table in a bar in Hua Hin, Thailand. They're the eyes of Paul McQueen. They're eyes that have seen things we weren't meant to see. Things nobody should *have* to see. They're the eyes of someone who's lost too much.

I pull my cigarettes from my pocket, slip a damp one from the pack and try to light it, but the wick of the lighter is too wet to catch.

The Zippo just sparks in the dark interior of the truck.

"You got one of those for me?" The young soldier asks. He slips a box of matches from a chest pocket and lights mine, then gratefully accepts a smoke with a crafty smile. "Don't tell on me, OK?" he chuckles, cupping the cigarette and ducking in his seat to make sure the driver of the truck behind can't see. "End of the world, and we're still not allowed to smoke on duty."

The truck turns off the freeway and onto a curved slip road, and I gaze out of the back in wonder. Beside the road I see buildings. Houses, stores, restaurants and gas stations, all with their lights on as if this was just a regular night. There are even a few cars on the roads, just driving along at regular speeds.

I can't fathom it. Ten miles away New York is a smoldering ruin, but here life is just humming along like always. There might even be people out there who don't know what's going on yet. People who stopped to fill up the car or grab a bite to eat after a day on the road, completely oblivious to the fact that the world as they know it is over. I envy them these few blissful moments of ignorance. I feel jealous that they get to to enjoy a little more time believing that tomorrow will hold no more surprises than a new episode of Game of Thrones.

To my right a new sight looms. Row upon row of military aircraft line up alongside passenger jets, behind which sit banks of olive green tents bathed in floodlights. It takes me a moment to figure out where we are, and my guess is confirmed when we pass beneath a large sign: *Welcome to Newark International Airport.*

"Refugee camp?" I ask, flicking my ash casually out the back of the truck as if I see vast military camps every day.

The soldier nods and smiles. "Yep. I guess this is where we'll be calling home for a while. The airspace is closed, so you'll be living right on the runway. Pretty cool, huh?" His smile fades. "I mean not cool. Just... well, you know what I mean."

Bishop climbs to the back of the truck as we turn through an open security gate and drive onto the vast runway. He stares out at the scene like a giddy kid, mouth open and eyes wide as we pass dozens of rows of long tents, their open doors revealing dozens of camp beds in each. The tents never seem to end. I stop counting as we pass the twentieth row, each of them at least five deep. By the look of it each tent must hold at least a hundred people, so just those tents I've seen so far are enough to house 10,000, and still the truck passes ever more.

"How many people got out?" I ask, my voice weak.

The soldier flicks his butt out the back of the truck and shakes his head. "Some. Not as many as we hoped. We're setting up three of these places around the state, but I guess they won't be more than half full. It all just happened too quickly, you know?"

The truck rolls to a halt beside a tent emblazoned with a red cross, and the soldier nods towards the door. "They'll take care of you guys from here. Looks like you'll need a few stitches."

I reach up to my head and wince as my fingers reach the gash on my forehead. I keep forgetting about it. "So, what happens now?"

"Now?" The soldier shrugs, and looks out over the endless bank of tents floodlit in the darkness. "Your guess is as good as mine, buddy. But I don't think it's all over." He jumps down from the truck and reaches out a hand. "Something tells me it's gonna get a lot worse before it get better."

I hop down to the asphalt, clenching my teeth at the pain in my legs, and wait for Bishop to climb down behind me. "Worse?" I look back in the direction of New York. In the dim moonlight I can still see the tower of smoke climbing high into the sky from the ruined city. "How could it get worse?"

The soldier shrugs, climbs back beneath the canvas canopy of the truck and taps the side until the driver begins to move. "Don't tempt fate, buddy. Good luck."

"Yeah," I whisper, almost to myself. As the truck pulls away I feel Bishop's arm slip around my shoulder to support me, and he pulls me in the direction of the medical tent. In the distance I see rows of trucks pull onto the runway, each of them carrying what few survivors could be found.

How can this possibly get any worse?

****

Follow Me

Thank you for reading HUNGER, the first book in the Last Man Standing series. The second book, CORDYCEPS, is available now exclusively at Amazon.

If you'd like to keep updated with my latest releases and sales you should subscribe to my newsletter:

https://app.mailerlite.com/webforms/landing/y1i5k1

or follow me on Facebook:

https://www.facebook.com/keithtaylorauthor

Book Two: CORDYCEPS

One Month On, A Nation Expects
Published May 4th, 2019 to the New York
Times website
Byline: Editorial Staff

In what's been described as the most
extensive mass migration event in the
nation's history, the month since the 4/7
attacks on New York City and Washington,
D.C. has seen millions flee west from the
once crowded eastern seaboard, both to
escape the immediate economic impact of
the disaster and to allay fears of further
attacks on major metropolitan centers.

An estimated 27 million refugees - almost
half the population of the now quarantined
northeastern region - have already escaped to
sparsely populated areas of Missouri,
Kentucky, Kansas and as far west as Oregon
in an exodus that has quickly overwhelmed
the capacity of municipal services, and local
governments have been left reeling under the

pressure to provide everything from emergency housing and medical care to basic food and potable water.

"We're calling Lexington 'Manhattan West'," jokes Maria Sloane, a mother of three who fled to Kentucky along with an estimated 85,000 former residents of Paterson, NJ, in what has been claimed by some to be an unnecessary economic migration. The group has been temporarily housed in an emergency camp established on the outskirts of the Daniel Boone National Forest, where efforts are under way to find a more permanent solution. "There's lots of money coming into these poor states. I don't really get why they're so mad about it."

While Sloane is correct in saying that the last month has seen an unprecedented injection of capital into struggling flyover states - both from the direct infusion of wealth from new arrivals and generous federal subsidies aimed at relieving the immense burden on regional governments - patience is beginning to wear thin among local residents, with many concerned about what will happen when the cash and good will finally runs dry.

"I don't mind the people from New York or D.C. at all," claims Boyd Wilson, manager of a bait shop on the outskirts of Lakeview Heights, KY. "Those folks really suffered. If a man loses his home I'll throw open my door and offer him a roof, no questions asked, but I just don't understand why we're expected to take in all these other people." Wilson complains that new arrivals from areas broadly unaffected by the attacks have been overfishing the local Triplett Creek, and that Cave Run Lake in the National Forest has become little more than a playground for wealthy easterners who don't respect the sacrifices made by local residents.

"Just last week I had a bunch in here looking for tips on where's the best fishing down at Phelps Branch on the Creek. That's a protected stretch, I told them. They need a special license to fish there, but they didn't give a hoot. And these were Boston folk, I could tell by their accents. There ain't no problems in Boston, far as I've heard. Why can't they just go home?"

Despite the local tensions most would admit that the United States has weathered the storm remarkably well in the aftermath of these unprecedented attacks, with leaders from the United Kingdom and much of Europe praising the difficult but decisive action taken to quell the danger, and the compassionate provision of aid to those affected, using lessons painfully learned from previous catastrophes such as Katrina and Sandy.

There have, however, been strong criticisms both at home and abroad of the heavy handed approach of law enforcement and recalled military forces, including accusations of racial profiling in Baltimore that led to the tragic loss of scores of lives in last week's food riots. There have also been ongoing constitutional questions regarding the legitimacy of the federal government in the light of President Howard's ongoing incapacity and the death of Vice President Lynch. Speaker Terrence Lassiter's accession to Acting President, while recognized as constitutionally valid at the time, has now been called into question by those who claim that the crisis is over, and argue that the reins should be handed back to a Democrat.

The Acting President's fitness to lead is no doubt further challenged by the fact that his government continues to operate from Site R, the secretive underground command post in the Raven Rock Mountain Complex north of Camp David. Detractors have called this an act of cowardice unbecoming of the office, and the fact that the Speaker was broadly disliked on both sides of the political divide even before the attacks leaves him with few allies in the corridors of power. Many commentators argue that the President's refusal to appear in public or even speak to the media in the past week severely erodes the argument that he is equipped to guide the nation through this ongoing crisis.

But what may prove the downfall of the Speaker and his government are not the tensions in the refugee-swamped central states, nor questions of the legitimacy or efficacy of his office, nor even the approaching economic disaster following a month of closed borders and stifled global trade, but the growing disquiet over the continued detention of US citizens in Newark Airport's Camp One. The camp, established on the day of the attacks to house refugees from New York City, has found itself at the center of a controversy not seen since the internment of American citizens of Japanese descent in the 1940s.

Those of us at the New York Times understand more than most the terrible realities of war. All of us lost friends, family and colleagues in the attack on New York, and all who survived the attacks, from the deputy editor in chief to the staff in the mail room, know that sacrifices must be made. We know that if our great nation is to survive these dark times we can't shy away from actions we may not consider palatable in peace time, but the time for transparency has come.

Our questions are simple and direct: will this government admit that upwards of eight thousand healthy, uninfected American citizens have been used as test subjects to develop a vaccine or cure for *Cordyceps bangkokii*? Will journalists, inspectors and other interested parties be given permission to enter Camp One to investigate these troubling claims, and will those detained at Newark Airport be permitted to speak publicly about their time there? If not, why not?

The citizens of the United States demand that these questions be answered. For too long has Speaker Lassiter's government remained silent on this urgent and pressing matter.

Grab your copy now

Printed in Great Britain
by Amazon